MACHINERY OF DEATH

The metal thing trembled, ever so slightly, and then set up a tremendous racket—whining, clanking, rattling, and whirring. Much to Bith's amazement, it began to walk across the room on its four hinged metal feet!

"Oh no!" Bith screamed. "You stop that, whatever you are!"

A thin metallic voice echoed around the tunnel:

"Do not disturb Arthana!"

A metal plate opened and out came a shiny arm with a sinister spike at the end. The spike touched Endril in the chest. There was a sizzle and hiss with a cloud of white smoke. Where the elf and the rat had been, there was now a seated skeleton, with a smaller one on its shoulder.

"Do not disturb Arthana!" droned the metallic voice as it reached out to Cal. . . .

Volume Six

THE STONE
OF TIME

Rose Estes and Tom Wham

ACE BOOKS, NEW YORK

THE STONE
OF TIME

CHAPTER
1
Revenge

The ominous cloud swirled heavily about the dark shapes that moved silently forward in the night. A cold autumn wind blew torrents of rain into their faces, and icy water trickled down through the gaps in their ragged cloaks. It froze into slush on their shoulders . . . but they did not complain. A flash of lightning briefly illuminated the scene and revealed hundreds of axe blades and spears pointing upward, and beneath the cloaks, thousands of cruel red glowing eyes. The Mistwall was on the move again, and these creatures of the darkness felt not the cold, for they were filled once more with the fire of victory.

An enormous war horse plodded among the figures, and its rider loomed above the others in the freezing blackness. Schlein was happy. More than merely happy. He was ecstatic. His thin blood coursed rapidly through his veins, his body quivering with the anticipation of a child awaiting a present. He could feel a song of victory building at the back of his throat. Death and destruction stretched in all directions as far as the eye could see. Even in the cold and rain, blood saturated the ground and the anguished cries of the dying rang in his ears like the crystal notes of some glorious song.

Torrents of black rain pelted the miserable defenders of the village of Cairngorm—those few who were unfortunate enough to still be alive—and a layer of freezing sleet coated the forms of the dead who would never rise again, their swords still clenched in their lifeless hands, cold steel trampled into the bloody frozen mud. The battle was in its final stages and none of Cairngorm would survive.

In the distance could be heard sporadic sounds of battle where Schlein's minions, those hideous battalions of orcs, goblins, and other unspeakable creatures were eradicating the last bits of human resistance. Around them all came the Mistwall, a sinuous curtain of writhing vapor that swallowed forever, whatever and whomever it encompassed. The village, and also Castle Cairngorm, had been valiantly defended by its loyal citizens, but, thanks to the workings of Schlein, their magic protection was gone . . . and the defense was now hopeless. Soon, all would be enveloped by the Mistwall.

Schlein rose in his stirrups. There was another flash of lightning and the huge magician was startled to see a small group of mounted knights, charging down upon him from a nearby hill in what seemed like slow motion. Schlein reached under his frost-covered fur cloak, pulled out a compact ebony wand, and pointed it in the direction of the impending attack.

"It's almost too easy," murmured the magician to himself with a smile. The sound of thundering hooves was now clearly audible above the din of battle and the noise of the storm. Schlein uttered a rhyming incantation, just as another flash revealed the knights almost upon him. A small ball of fire flew off the tip of the wand and grew into a massive roaring flame which enveloped the unfortunate horsemen before they could strike. When the smoke and fire had cleared, the few dazed survivors vanished under a solid wave of axe-wielding goblins.

The Second Battle of Cairngorm was over and done. The miserable village and those who had died defending it were now but a memory, swelling the Mistwall to slightly greater proportions and extending its black border of death. Schlein nodded to himself and stroked his blond beard, which had grown in nicely following his fiery encounter with the sorceress Elizebith of Morea. Were it not for her and her meddling cohorts, this worthless village would have been his long ago. Now its conquest gave him a satisfaction all out of proportion to its real importance in the grand scheme of things.

His thoughts returned to Elizebith. Schlein had managed to imprison the girl for a short time, in an effort to wed and bed her . . . a deed which would have greatly increased his own power while diminishing hers.

Unfortunately, things had not worked out the way he had planned and Elizebith had managed to escape, along with the elf Endril. The two had been aided in their effort by their companions—Hathor the troll and the boy warrior Caltus Talienson. Schlein marked these names well; they were at the top of his list. He had not climbed to the position of dark prominence, which he so enjoyed, by being soft and unforgiving. He was nothing if not a vengeful man. Only these four had bested him and lived to tell the tale; he did not intend to let this situation continue. The accursed companions, Bith and her friends, had managed to foil and escape him at every turn for the last two years. A mere moment in history, a brief moment, but he would see to it that they paid dearly, and with interest, for the discomfort they had caused him.

The massive man twisted in the saddle, and grimaced slightly at the pull of a stiffened muscle, marking the long hours he had sat astride his war horse, overseeing the destruction. His presence had not really been necessary; the duly required death and destruction could have been achieved without him, for the orcs and goblins had merely to be pointed in the right direction and loosed on their hapless opponents. They needed no supervision in how to kill. The hard part was getting them to stop. Once the blood lust set in, only exhaustion and the lack of victims could put an end to their wanton slaughter. It was not unheard of for them to fall upon each other, murdering their own kith and kin when their base desires were unslaked at the end of a battle. Fortunately that had not been the case here at Cairngorm, for the defenders had been massed six deep and there had been enough bloodshed to satisfy even the most savage of goblins.

Schlein reined in his horse at the top of a knoll. The rain had let up and an eerie blue glow lit up the field; it was almost dawn now. He stretched luxuriously in the saddle, smiling down at the orcs and goblins as they moved through the mounds of the dead, retrieving their spoils—weapons and clothing and whatever bits of finery caught their eye— and dispatching those few unlucky souls who had survived the carnage. Scavenging among the dead after a battle was, for the horrid army, like a sumptuous dessert following a banquet.

Such activities held no interest for Schlein, however, and he directed his horse toward a certain beechwood forest which stood a few leagues to the north. He rode alone in the receding darkness, along a narrow rutted path. His horse needed no urging; it feared its master, and sullenly plodded on through the freezing mud. At length the man and rider surmounted a low hill. The path led through a tiny village and then into a peaceful wood. Soon it would be peaceful no more. Schlein dismounted and strolled among the stately trees which rose above him in a graceful manner. Their white trunks were massive and bore the marks of great age. Here, there had been no rain, no sleet, and the Mistwall had not yet arrived. Battles and bloodshed meant next to nothing in such a place. Many battles had been won and lost in the long years that had passed since these proud tree-patriarchs were but tiny saplings, and there were few alive who even remembered why the battles had been fought.

The silvery leaves whispered above him, soft murmurings whose meanings Schlein was unable to decipher, although he was certain that there were those for whom the message was perfectly clear.

The forest had been a source of deep pleasure for the elf Endril, and had renewed his spirit and fortified his courage nightly as he wandered among its peaceful groves.

Endril was far away now, and on the ground layer upon layer of fallen leaves absorbed the sound of Schlein's passage as though the step of a mere mortal were incapable of making an imprint on that magic grove. Schlein lifted his face to a ray of morning sunlight and smiled at the thought. He would make his mark on this forest whether or not it approved of him. Its magic was powerful, but then, so was his, now.

Schlein rummaged in his pouch and withdrew two items: a craggy flint given to him (although not without persuasion) by a recalcitrant fire giant, and a striker forged by a master dwarf, which never failed to produce a spark. The wood fell silent. No bird sang; no leaf fluttered. Even the sunlight seemed to lose its warmth. Schlein smiled while the forest held its breath.

He looked around him, and a tiny twinge of pity pierced his breast as he realized the magnitude of what he was about to do, of the peace and beauty that would be lost forever. For a moment he almost stayed his hand, and then he shook off the aberrant thought, snarled hoarsely, and touched striker to flint. A single magical spark appeared, trembled, and then fell to the dry mast, where it glowed crimson, pulsing slightly as it fed, growing swiftly in strength and size.

Schlein stepped back as the tiny flames began to rise, crackling as they burned down through the centuries-thick carpet of fallen leaves.

The trees seemed to shrink back in horror from the flames, but enchanted though they were, they were incapable of flight, and in the end they burned just like any other bit of wood. The sap, the lifeblood of the birches, steamed and boiled and bubbled up through thousands of tiny cracks, uttering shrill wails of anguish. The trunks swayed and moaned in agony, and the silvery leaves writhed and twisted in torment as they were consumed by the flames.

Schlein remounted quickly and his horse, its eyes rolling in terror, bolted out the far side of the forest and raced up the side of a nearby hill where it stood with bowed head and heaving flanks, trembling from more than the considerable weight of its rider.

Schlein tightened his grip on the reins and watched as the billowing clouds of smoke boiled upward, merging with the impenetrable blackness of the swiftly advancing Mistwall. Cairnwald, the enchanted forest, had kept Schlein and the Dark Lord at bay, unable to advance their foul cloud either forward or around it. The destruction of the forest was inevitable, part of the larger plan. Then too, it had given succor to his opponent, and one of the basic strategies of warfare was to destroy anything, any place, and anyone that might aid the enemy.

Still, as Schlein gazed upon the destruction he had wrought, witnessing the last of the forest fall beneath the flames, its beauty and serenity gone forever, something moved inside him, and he twisted uneasily as he was swept with sorrow and remorse. He had not always been so cold, so heartless, so dedicated to evil. Once, he had been different. . . . Schlein closed his eyes, and in spite of himself, remembered a long dead past . . . a woman with green eyes, and long, flowing red hair. . . .

A fearful orc tugged at his stirrup and broke the spell.

"What is it?" Schlein roared, over the din of the fire. He raised his hand to swat at the intruder, who cowered low and handed up a battered scroll with a trembling claw. The wizard grabbed the parchment, and the orc quickly scampered off into the confusion of the fire and disappeared. Schlein shook his head to clear it of thoughts of the past. He couldn't understand what had come over him.

He unrolled the scroll. New orders from the Dark Lord himself. Schlein grunted, wondering what had gone wrong, and turned his mount away from the fires and headed back to camp.

CHAPTER
2
Evil Tidings

Endril awoke with a start and looked around him. He had fallen asleep against a tall oak tree, and there was frost on the leaves of the forest floor. Stiff and chilled, he slapped his shoulders to restore his circulation as he arose in the red glow of early morning light. The first frost of the year. He should be enjoying this . . . but there was something undefinable that was troubling him. It was just a feeling, but it persisted, gnawing at the back of his mind.

The elf crunched his way through the wood, his feet breaking through the thin layer of ice that had formed on the forest litter. He turned left at the creek and started back toward the manor where his companions were staying. He shivered, watching his breath in the crisp morning air, and the thought of the warm fire at the lodge was very appealing.

A great house with rows of arched windows, and several pointed spires stood at the base of the next rise, and Endril hurried down the path. Smoke poured out of the chimneys, and the welcome smells of breakfast came to him on the cool morning air. He pushed open the kitchen door and found himself among a throng of bustling cooks.

"Good morrow, Master Endril," said Bertha, the woman in charge, as she stirred a great iron kettle with a large wooden spoon. "Spent the night in the wood again, did ye?"

The elf forced the frown on his face into a smile, waved, and then pushed on into the dining hall. The large room was so dimly lit at this time of the morning that the elf could barely make out one of the servants putting logs on the fire. Endril made his way silently to the hearth, and then addressed the man.

"Good morning, Sam!"

The man dropped his bundle of logs on the floor with a clatter. "Oh, 'tis you, Master Endril, You gave me quite a start, you did!" The man set about gathering up his load from the stone hearth, and Endril lent a hand. "I be edgy ever since awakenin' this morn. I canna ken what is the matter wi' me." Sam threw a log into the fire, and a spray of sparks bounced out onto the stones. "There be somethin' wrong but I jus' canna put me finger on it!"

"I know how you feel," replied the elf. "There's something wrong. I can feel it too." He moved closer to the flames and rubbed his hands together while Sam put the rest of the wood into the fire and then poked at the logs with a long stick.

"Mebbe that 'ere Mistwall is gobblin' up another kingdom summ'ere," ventured the man, glancing sideways at Endril.

The elf nodded silently. "I fear you may be right; there's evil afoot!" He turned toward the front door, paused for a moment, and then made up his mind. "Tell my companions, when they arise, that I have gone to the crossroads to seek news."

"Aye, sir!" Sam replied, raising his hand to his forehead in a kind of salute. The elf walked silently across the hall to the door and was gone without a sound.

• • •

Elizebith of Morea stood rubbing her hands together beside the fire. Her silver eyes shone brightly in contrast to the long raven-colored hair that flowed down the back of the shimmering black dress that she always wore. Seated nearby was the troll Hathor and the boy warrior Caltus. Bith was worried about Endril; he had been gone too long. She turned to her companions with her hands on her hips.

"Cal, I want you to ride out to the crossroads and see if he's all right."

The boy was not keen on the idea, having just finished an enormous meal. Relaxation was all that was on his mind. "That elf can take care of himself. You know how he is when he takes on one of his moods. . . ."

"No!" insisted the dark-haired girl, stomping her foot for emphasis. "Get up now, and go check on him!" Bith reached over, grabbed Cal by the collar, and yanked him unceremoniously to his feet.

"Okay! All right, already. I'll go!" answered the reluctant boy.

"And go to the kitchen and fetch him some food too," declared the girl. "Endril's been out there for a day now with nothing to eat."

"Yeah, sure!" came Cal's grouchy answer as he skulked off toward the door, grumbling beneath his breath.

"I swear, I don't know what's gotten into him," said Bith as the door slammed shut.

"Too much food!" said Hathor from his place by the hearth. "He know his duty. He take food, get news. . . ." The troll looked into Elizebith's worried face. "I go too?"

"No, no, Thor," replied the girl, wrapping her arms about her shoulders and sitting again before the fire. "I'm just edgy, like everyone else around here. And I fear that the news, when it comes, will not be good."

The troll edged forward, placed his mighty paw on her fragile shoulder, and gave the girl a reassuring pat.

• • •

Endril leaned against the signpost and watched as yet
another ragtag band of refugees hurried along the road. He
finished the last bit of bread from the bag of food Cal had
brought him the night before and dropped the sack to the
ground. Last night, there had been no news, good or bad,
but now things had changed. His expression was troubled.

All morning long he had watched the road, and the
steady flow of travelers, all pouring out of the north, was
not a good sign. Most of the refugees had panicked at the
sight of his dark, solitary figure, and had fled in terror
into the woods before he was able to speak to them. No
ordinary travelers, these, they included whole families with
their possessions piled helter-skelter atop creaking wagons,
with milk cows, goats, and pigs tied on behind and crates
of chickens clucking their dismay.

Finally, after several frustrating hours, he was able to
approach an old man pulling a cart, who had stopped and
was seated on a rock, too exhausted to run from the elf.
The news he told was dire indeed.

Endril was shocked to discover that some of the refugees
were among those few residents who had survived the
destruction of the village of Cairngorm and the nearby
village of Cairnwald. To his sorrow he also learned of
Schlein's destruction of the beautiful beechwood forest.
Endril closed his eyes and pressed a hand to his chest,
feeling the pain deep within. It was always so when something died, but there was no greater pain than the death of
a forest caused by a wanton hand.

The oldster, unsettled by the elf's grief, and anxious to
be on his way, quickly related the advance of the Mistwall,
telling how it had swallowed his ancestral farm and how he
had fled for his life, and of those unfortunates who had not
been quick enough to do so.

Endril had been unable to speak, numbed by the news of
the swift advance of the Dark Lord. How had it happened
so quickly? The exhausted old man picked up the shafts of

his cart and hurried away with many a backward glance. A swaybacked, sharp-hipped milch cow tied to the end of the cart rolled her eyes at Endril and lowed piteously, perhaps mourning the loss of her familiar stall.

Endril stood and watched until the forlorn duo passed over the rim of the hill and vanished from sight. Only then did he turn his gaze in the direction from which they had come, the direction of Cairngorm. He stared intently, and there it was, dark clouds billowing up from the edge of the horizon into the sky, obliterating everything from view. Those were not ordinary storm clouds, which would have their moment of violence and then vanish, but something far more ominous, with far-reaching implications. They boiled and surged as though alive, the outer skin of some ravenous beast who would consume the very world itself if given the opportunity.

Endril shivered and drew his cloak more tightly about him, knowing that the image was not far wrong. The Mistwall was a manifestation of the Dark Lord, whose intention it was to bring the entire world under his dark rule. The Mistwall had advanced rapidly, and in the struggle of good against evil on this sad morning, it appeared that the Dark Lord was winning.

At last, Endril turned his back on the awful vision and walked slowly down the empty road to the manor where he and his three friends were guests. His news would not be welcome.

The elf's companions were at the dining table, halfway through the evening meal when he entered the room. Elizebith of Morea, raven-haired sorceress, was seated across from Caltus Talienson, boy warrior, and the strong and steady troll Hathor. The four of them, once outcasts, now seemed destined to fight against the Dark Lord for the rest of their lives. The elf had not eaten since morning but, at the moment, all thoughts of food had vanished. He told his friends of the fall of Cairnwald, the magic place where they had spent an almost idyllic winter of rest.

"But how can this be?" Bith asked, shocked and upset. "When we left Cairngorm it was safe in the hands of the villagers. And Cairnwald was protected by a magic spell. . . ."

"Not enough," Hathor said tersely. "Them not strong enough to hold. Spell broken. Dark One win."

Endril walked closer to the fire, with a pained look on his face. "Things have been too quiet for too long, and once again, we have been caught napping. While we rested on our laurels, the Dark Lord has been busy."

"I'll wager it's the work of Schlein again," snapped Bith angrily. "Who else would lead the Dark Lord's forces back into Cairngorm? That evil beast has caused us more than our share of troubles."

"I would imagine that our old nemesis is, indeed, the power behind this," said the elf rather matter-of-factly. "Burning Cairnwald would give him great satisfaction. The place protected us from him for so long."

"And Malendor is no more!" said Cal, sitting up in his chair. It had not been long since Schlein had fallen into disfavor and the Dark Lord had called upon Endril's old enemy Malendor, an undead elf with hideous power. Yet the four present had easily disposed of Malendor. . . . "Who else remains to lead the Dark Lord's forces?"

"New foe," suggested Hathor. "Worse than Schlein or Malendor."

"No! Only Schlein would burn Cairnwald." Cal pushed his chair back and stood up. "It looks like war again, and we four are called to action." The boy warrior flexed his arms, feeling the muscles move under the skin, reassured by the simple matter of his own healthy existence. He unsheathed his sword, and moving apart from the small group, began a series of moves calculated to stir the blood and quicken the responses. "No sense brooding about it," he said as he went through the graceful motions, his blade cutting the smoky air of the room. "There's nothing we could have done to prevent this from happening. If we had been there, we'd likely have been swallowed by the Mistwall as well. Now there's nothing left to do but fight."

Bith watched the play of Cal's muscles with fascination, once again aware of her increasing attraction to the boy warrior, an interest that had grown, against her will, ever more powerful since his ill-fated romance with Yvaine. The girl gave herself a mental shake and turned her eyes away, frowning at the gleam of amusement in Hathor's eyes. "Well, what are we to do?" she asked.

"Roanwood lies several leagues distant," replied Endril. "We can make it by midday if we start in the morning. Or by midnight if we start now. Perhaps we will learn more along the way."

"Better make it tomorrow," said the girl, "I must pack, and we have to bid farewell to our gracious host. Lord Rotherham will be quite put out if we leave without a word."

"Perhaps he can lend us horses." added Cal.

"Indeed I shall," said a deep voice from the far end of the hall. It was Lord Rotherham himself, and he approached the four companions on unsteady legs, tapping a walking stick with each step. "I knew action would be your choice when trouble came again. Not only shall you have horses, but I'll see to it that you have plenty of food for your journey." The bent old man leaned on his cane in front of the table. "Were I not so old and feeble, I too would go with you."

"We are all most grateful for your help," said Bith, with a smile that melted the old man's heart.

"Yet you should not leave blindly without a course of action. I would counsel you to go to the court of King Ethelrud. News I have had from there would lead me to believe he is calling together all those on this side of the dreaded Mistwall, to form a grand alliance to stop the Dark Lord."

The four companions and their noble host walked over to the fire and discussed options and plans. Bith spent much time thanking Lord Rotherham for his hospitality. Since their victory over the Dark Lord at Trondholm, the four heroes had stayed as guests at a succession of noble houses. Their mere presence brought honor and prestige to their hosts. Lord Rotherham had been different, taking none of the glory and giving freely of himself. Their stay had been most pleasant, if too short.

The group talked well into the night, until, at last, near midnight, the old man fell asleep in his chair. Cal noticed the lord's closed eyes and motioned to the others.

"I think our host is talked out," he whispered.

"We'd better get some rest ourselves," said Bith as she stood up and walked over to the old man. The girl kissed him gently on the forehead, and then she, Hathor, Cal—and for once Endril—retired to their rooms, some to sleep, and the rest to restlessly ponder what the future held in store.

CHAPTER
3

A Summons

Rotherham was better than his word, and at sunrise the heroes found themselves presented with four magnificent war horses, and three strong mules to bear their gear. Bith's services were required to calm the horses, so that Hathor could even approach the animals, let alone mount. Trolls and horses do not ordinarily mix, but a spell taught to Bith by the dwarf Gunnar Greybeard did the trick, and soon all the animals were nuzzling up to the red-haired troll and he grinned with embarrassment.

The air was crisp and cold, and the sky a brilliant blue. The gathering loom of the Mistwall, now just over the horizon, was fortunately hidden by the tall trees to the west. The manor staff had turned out to see the four companions off. A crowd of shivering servants and guests gathered together for warmth on the front lawn while Lord Rotherham stood on the high marble steps making a rather long-winded speech before the final farewells. Once again he cautioned them to travel to the court of Ethelrud, King of the Westwoods, for counsel before they took any action against the Dark Lord.

At last the speech was over, and the crowd let out a feeble

huzzah. Cal flung his cloak over his shoulder and led off,
pointing his fine horse out the gravel path that made toward
the crossroads. He turned back to look at the crowd, and
they cheered, this time in earnest. The boy warrior waved
and then prodded his mount into a trot. The great house
and its spires disappeared behind the crest of the hill, and
the four heroes of Cairngorm, those who slew the Queen of
Ice, the Conquerors of Murcroft, the Victors of Trondholm,
rode on to what would surely be yet another duel with the
Dark Lord.

During the long evening chat with Lord Rotherham, the
group had secretly resolved to ignore the old man's warning
and proceed directly toward the Mistwall to face Schlein.
Hathor rode silently in the rear, uneasy in his saddle despite
the spell cast on the horses by Bith. The troll was bothered
most, however, by the headstrong manner in which his
companions were rushing toward action without any real
plan. Even though he had no runesword, Cal had blathered
on about duty, honor, and confidence. Elizebith had bragged
that her magic was equal or better now than that of Schlein.
Endril was enraged by the destruction of Cairnwald, and
seemed to have lost all reason . . . so, outnumbered, Hathor
had silently acquiesced, knowing that any objections he
might raise would be met with scorn.

By the time the group reached the crossroads and turned
west, grey clouds had rolled across the sky and the tem-
perature dropped. The breath of the horses emerged as
great plumes of white mist as the animals snorted nervously in the gathering gloom. On the main road, the four
found themselves riding past a steady stream of refugees,
some with carts and wagons, but most on foot, fleeing the
blackening menace of the Mistwall, which was advancing
across the free world. The wind picked up and whistled
through the evergreens, sending a chill down Hathor's back.
He hunched down under his bearskin cloak and wished that
he had a crisp root to munch on.

Occasionally, Cal or Endril would stop a passerby in an effort to gain information on just what it was they were likely to find ahead. Bith remained unusually silent, intent upon a small book, given her at parting by Lord Rotherham—a book from which she hardly lifted her eyes. Hathor too, remained silent, and to keep his mind from the Mistwall, dreamed of food.

By midday, they had reached Roanwood, a small dense forest that was skirted on the north by the road they had followed. Cal and Endril talked for a moment and then led the horses into the shelter of some trees where the four stopped to confer and eat a bit of lunch.

"Those two men I just spoke to," said Cal, leaning against a tree, "were soldiers from the Duchy of Glenn. An entire army of men has been destroyed."

"Then it is not just Cairngorm which has fallen?" asked Bith, finally looking up from her book.

"No, the alliance sent forth an army as soon as the trouble began." Cal put a bottle of wine to his lips and drank, then wiped his lips with his sleeve. "Now it is destroyed. It looks as though we are the only hope."

Hathor could remain silent no longer, and looked into the boy warrior's eyes, "You say we go fight! You say we last hope!" The troll turned to Elizebith, "You say your magic powerful now!" Hathor then turned to Endril. "We do not practice. We do not discuss. What is plan?"

The elf smiled and patted the troll on the shoulder, "Well put, my friend. At the moment we have no plan, but I am confident that as we near the enemy, something will come to us."

"Perhaps Vili will come to us with advice," suggested Bith. She had put away her mysterious book and was now picking at a cold roast hen.

"That thought had crossed my mind, too," remarked Cal.

"Hope so!" grumbled the troll, who then pulled a fist full of roots out of a brown sack and began crunching noisily on a particularly large red one.

The cold meal was soon finished and they returned to the road. The black cloud that was the Mistwall merged in the distance with the grey overcast so that all seemed one great blur, and the Wall seemed to draw closer even as they urged their horses in its general direction. Again the four passed one group of refugees after another, all of whom told their own version of the disaster.

By mid-afternoon they overtook a strange wagon which was also traveling in the direction of the Mistwall. It was drawn by a team of six fine horses, and was heaped with grain which could barely be seen, for it in turn was covered by a wriggling swarm of furry black, grey, and brown creatures. Above all, waved a multitude of long, thin tails. The man who held the reins was himself covered with the creatures.

Hathor shook his head in amazement. Endril let out a little shout of joy, nudged his horse to a gallop, and rode ahead to talk. Bith looked up, took in the loaded wagon, and let out a shriek.

It was a wagonload of rats. Rats in all sizes and colors. Rats rode on the brim of the driver's hat like the figurehead of a ship. Sniffling rat noses poked out of his pockets, several tails snaked out the neck of his shirt, and bright eyes peeked over the edge of his shoulder, diving beneath his vest as Endril rode alongside. Now, ordinarily this would be an unusual sight, in any place, at any time, but not so for Endril. The elf had spent many days in a dungeon with the driver of this wagon, and with the rats as well. The rats, in fact, had provided Endril and Bith with the means of escaping from Schlein's grasp, not more than a year before, and now the creatures were honored, if not welcome, around the land.

"Purkins!" the elf cried happily, overjoyed to find that his friend, who had shared the cell in Murcroft's dungeon, was on the same road, going in the same direction.

The man in the hat covered with rats hunched over and glanced sideways. The dark, angry expression on his face vanished as soon as he recognized the elf.

"Endril!" he shouted, hauling back on the reins, bringing the team up, short and sending a wave of rats and grain sliding forward. "Endril, old friend, never did I think to see you again!" He looked back into the pile of grain and rats and called out, "Blackie, look who's here!"

One of the rats, a fat black fellow with a sleek pelt and long shiny whiskers, climbed out of the mound and jumped, somewhat heavily, onto Purkin's shoulder. This was no ordinary rat, either, for he had been charmed for life by the dwarf Gunnar Greybeard, and now spoke the language of men. "Hey, it's our friends from the tower! I din't think we'd see ya again so soon! Bad news this Mistwall business, huh! An' jus' when I thought things was gonna get good! Oh, well, it's still a whole lot more excitin' than bein' back home."

"We only learned recently of the fall of Cairngorm," said Endril. "But tell me, why are you all on the road, and what's more, traveling in what is obviously the wrong direction?"

"Well, climb aboard," said Purkins, dusting off the bench beside him, sending another wave of rats scurrying. "We have only a small distance more to travel, and I like not the way that evil wall is gaining on our path."

Looking up, Endril could only agree; the Mistwall seemed closer than ever. Grasping the edge of the wagon, the elf dropped from his saddle onto the seat beside Purkins and tied the reins of his horse to a metal fitting. Hathor and Cal rode up and made their hellos but preferred to stay mounted, as did Bith, who forced out a greeting of sorts and then directed her mount to the far side of Cal, putting distance between herself and the rats. They may have saved her life once, but they still gave her the creeps.

Purkins made a clucking noise and the six horses lurched forward in unison, pulling the wagonload of grain and rats forward along the bumpy road.

"The boys and I," said the driver, "and by boys, I mean our furry friends here, are on a kind of secret mission." Purkins leaned back and shoved his arm elbow-deep into the pile of grain. A moment later he pulled out a shiny gold bar and twirled it about in his hand.

"Hey," screamed Blackie the rat. "Put that back under; you never know who might be lookin'! Ya wanna blow our cover?"

"Okay! Okay!" Purkins said sheepishly, and he shoved the gold back into the pile of grain. The rat hopped down and proceeded to bury the treasure more securely with a flurry of tiny feet and a spray of kicked-up grain.

The driver turned to Endril. "We have to deliver this gold to a bunch of ogres in a cave up the road a ways."

"Ogres?" asked Cal in amazement. "Why ogres? Don't they work for the Dark Lord?"

"I thought it was a funny idea, too," remarked Purkins. "But, heck, this fancy lot of riders came into my stable the other day . . . said they come from King Ethel—"

"Ethelrud," prompted Endril.

"Yeah Ethelrud, that's the name! Anyway, they said they'd give me three o' them gold bars if I'd take the rest to these ogres in the Cave of Casneer. Well, I asked 'em why, an' they said them ogres would work for anyone if the price was right!" Purkins reached into his vest and pulled out a crumpled roll of paper. "The deal is all here on this scroll, I guess."

"Well, I sure hope you've got enough there to convince those ogres," said Cal with a smile. The boy turned to the troll. "Now, Hathor, see. What did I tell you? Things are already looking up. We've run into an old friend, and he is about to buy us some allies."

Even Elizebith seemed cheerful, and looked up again from her book. "What's more, Thor, this book given me by Rotherham is a spellbook he's had in his family for generations. I'm learning a lot of new tricks."

Hathor shook his head. "Believe, when I see."

• • •

Ethelrud, crown ruler of the three Kingdoms of West-wood, and nominal head of all forces that opposed the Dark Lord, drew a shaking hand down over his eyes, shielding them for a brief moment from the piteous sight of the streams of refugees, visible through every window of the castle, clogging the roads as far as the eye could see. The king's sad eyes and stooped shoulders gave testament to the fact that the task ahead of him was monumental.

"Well, what shall we do next, Geoffry," asked the king, turning to his companion, Geoffry of Glencoe, a short, slender man who was seated next to Ethelrud. "Now that our wizards have failed at Cairnwald, Hamm, and Kilmorec, and three armies have been destroyed?" It was not so much a question as it was a statement of failure. Geoffry shook his head sadly and remained silent. The others present grumbled in unison and twisted uneasily in their seats.

This was no ordinary gathering, but a convocation of the most powerful kings, princes, dukes, and landowners in all the world. Many of those seated around the table had already lost their kingdoms and in many instances, loved ones, to the Mistwall. And those whose lands had yet to be threatened knew that it was but a matter of time before they too fell to the inexorable advance of the dark cloud. No longer could they deny the threat which many of them had scoffed at only a short time before.

They had assembled here at the Castle Glencoe, in the Middle Kingdom of Westwood, by mutual accord, bringing with them their armies and their personal magicians, spellcasters, and scryers in an attempt to find a final solution, a plan, a way to defeat the Dark Lord. To a man, they were willing and ready to fight for their lands, but how did one fight a cloud? A relentless advancing cloud that concealed vile armies of foul creatures, its march was more deadly and unmerciful than that of any living army, and what it took, it did not surrender. Lands, buildings, crops, livestock, and even people, were swallowed whole by the Mistwall—a cloud into which no one could travel with hope of return. Any fight, any battle, any last stand, would have to be made on this side of the Mistwall, for there was no way to penetrate the Realms of the Dark Lord.

Suddenly the silence was broken.

"Fire," said Moorlock, crown prince of the vanished Duchy of Natwick, his fists clenched tightly upon the gleaming tabletop. "Let us set a row of fires to burning across the Mistwall's path. Surely that will stop it."

Geoffry of Glencoe bestowed a soft and pitying glance on the young prince, who had lost parents, siblings, and his sweetheart to the Mistwall. "Fire will have no effect, young Moorlock, for it has surely swallowed many hundreds of cook fires, hearth fires, and bonfires in its advance, with no noticeable effect."

"Not to mention the great fire set at the city of Hamm," added a fat, bearded man at the far side of the table. "The whole city was consumed with flame, yet it seemed only to feed the Mistwall even more. This I saw with my own eyes!"

"True, Lord Kurrok," said Geoffry in a somber voice. "And I know how it pains you to tell us of that fire." Then, turning back to the others, he stated firmly, "The element of fire will not save us from the Dark Lord."

The young king of Glencoe was destined for great things someday. His mild and retiring manner masked a keen mind and brilliant intellect which often as not saw at a glance what it took other minds far longer to assimilate. Considered by many of his contemporaries to be the foremost tactician and master of warfare, his opinion of the crisis which confronted them was eagerly awaited by all of those gathered around the long banquet table.

"Well, what then!" cried another, bringing his fists down hard on the tabletop. "We cannot just sit here and talk while that . . . that vile thing is eating our entire world!"

"True, we must do something, but the question is what?" replied Geoffry. "None of the conventional methods of warfare seem to have any effect on it at all. We have tried everything we know to do. Now, all that is left is to capitulate . . ."

A roar went up around the table, and as one voice those in attendance shouted, "Never!"

When the noise subsided, Geoffry continued. "You didn't let met finish: Capitulate or . . ."

"Or what?" blurted out the impatient Prince Moorlock of Natwick as Geoffry hesitated.

"Or we alter time!" All fell silent. Geoffry went on, "We alter time and change the very nature of history, so that the Dark Lord never existed."

"Ridiculous!" scoffed one of the many kings present, "How can this possibly be done? Modify time, indeed." There was a general murmur of agreement, and Geoffry could see that more explanation was needed. The young king pushed back his chair and began walking slowly around the circle of noblemen and kings. "I have long been in consultation with the mages of the land, and one, Greenlock is his name, has been to the mythical city of Abaton. You've heard of it, of course?"

All present shook their heads.

Geoffry continued. "Then perhaps you have seen this city; it is only visible near sunset, and it . . ."

A gleam appeared in the narrow beady eyes of one of the kings, who stood up and interrupted the speaker. " . . . it is seen only at sunset and its spires are just visible over the horizon."

Geoffry smiled. "And within Abaton may be found the fabled Stone of Time . . . *whosoever possesses the stone may go back and alter events before they have happened.*"

"But nobody has ever been able to reach Abaton," protested the beady-eyed king. "As you approach, the city remains just over the horizon. We shall never be able to get to the place, let alone use your 'fabled stone'!"

Geoffry continued his circuit of the table. "Quite so, Quite so. For most of us, even our best magician, reaching the city of Abaton is quite beyond our powers." He stopped and raised a finger into the air.

"But there are those in the land who have performed virtually one miracle after another. Those who have snatched victory time and again from the hands of the Dark Lord and his minions."

"The four heroes . . ." whispered someone several places down.

"Yes, the four heroes," said the young king, folding his arms across his chest. "Send for those who stopped the cloud at Cairngorm, slew the Queen of Ice, and who saved Trondholm. If any among us can do this deed, they are the ones. Perhaps with the Stone of Time they can work a more lasting miracle and banish the horrible Mistwall once and for all."

"I too have heard of this, this Abaton, but I never believed in that tale," said Moorlock of Natwick. "And now you would send a troll, an elf, a girl, and a boy to save the world." Moorlock frowned skeptically.

"We have no choice," said Geoffry, "other than to pray that the story about the Stone is true and that the four heroes will find the answer. While they wrestle with the Dark Lord in the long dead past, we shall send what remains of our armies to deal with him in the present. And maybe, just maybe, it will work. I know not what else to do, for we have tried every other means."

"And I say *no!*" A tall, balding man dressed in plain grey robes stood up and waved his fist in the air. "Those *heroes* you speak of are nothing but glory seekers. They have taken advantage of good fortune to claim honor for themselves. They can be of no use to us!"

"But what else would you suggest!" cried another noble seated nearby.

"Raise an even larger army," shouted a burly monarch. "Conscript everyone—the peasants, the artisans, everyone. Leave the cities vacant!"

"I agree with Geoffry. Send for the four heroes!"

"Never!"

A lengthy debate broke out among the rulers, some arguing for and others against. Repeatedly, Geoffry had to restate his plan and in the end none could come up with a better one. Soon all attention returned to Geoffry.

"Who among you is willing to ride out with me in search of these four? We must bring them here!"

"Then it is I who will go with you," cried young Moorlock, leaping to his feet so swiftly that his chair crashed to the floor behind him.

Geoffry nodded his approval, and his eyes scanned the others who sat round the table. The Meister of Ballwick was too old for the journey, and Enteric of Mersewood was too stout to sit on his horse for long periods of time. Warfield was solid and could be relied upon to do what he had set out to do, but he was needed here to maintain order over the townspeople, the landowners, and the massed armies.

One after another, Geoffry discarded this prince and that lord for various reasons, until in the end, there remained only young Moorlock. Too young, too inexperienced, and too filled with anger to be entrusted with such an important mission, he was nevertheless the obvious choice.

"Then it is decided! Young Moorlock and I shall go." Geoffry turned to Warfield. "I trust you to look after the organization of the new army, and you may count on Ethelrud for all cooperation and assistance."

At that moment, King Ethelrud, who had remained silent throughout the proceedings, finally rose and spoke. "I cannot impress upon you enough the need for secrecy in what we are planning here. If word of our plans reaches the Dark Lord, the free world as we know it is doomed!"

The king called for a toast, and servants rushed in with glasses and decanters of wine. They drank to success and to the health of all present, then tossed their glasses into the fire. No one noticed that the glass belonging to the tall bald man in the grey robes had gone untouched.

• • •

Geoffry sighed and passed a hand over the silky white-blond strands of hair that hovered halo-like around his head. He had hoped to avoid this journey out of concern for his own young wife and child. But who better than he knew the importance of this mission? If the four were not found, there would be no place left on earth that would be safe. For the sake of his wife and daughter, he could do nothing other than go. He could only hope that Alison, his gentle wife, would understand, for he had not mentioned the trip to her as yet.

Master tactician and king he might be, but he was also a husband, and, at home, it was his wife who ruled supreme. Throughout the remainder of that day and long into the night, the council pieced together the bits of knowledge and gossip concerning the odd foursome. Scryers peered into their crystals, and two magicians cast seeing spells which brought forth odorous clouds of smoke. The land was searched to discover the whereabouts of Hathor, Endril, Elizebith, and Cal. Finally, near dawn, one of the scryers, a doddering ancient with filmed eyes and long, skeletal fingers, uttered a cry that wakened many of those who slumped over the table or slumbered in their chairs.

"I have found them!" he quavered exultantly, his long, sensitive fingers drifting over the surface of the cloud-filled globe. "They are here, on the road near Roanwood, and I see . . . I see . . ." The old man shook his head in disbelief.

"What do you see?" demanded an impatient Moorlock.

"I see rats . . . ." said the old scryer, now smiling. "Many scores of rats." His feeble voice faltered as though he doubted his vision, but then it grew firm. "Yes, they are there. Roanwood is where you will find them. And the rats."

Late though the hour, Geoffry and Moorlock took their leave of those gathered round the table and made their way to the courtyard. Normally deserted at such an hour, the place was now crowded to capacity with soldiers and villagers whose homes had been consumed by the Mistwall. Bonfires burned brightly all around the perimeter of the walls as well as on the cobblestones.

Horses whinnied and stamped nervously, soldiers coughed and came to attention as their anxious eyes followed the passage of the king among them. Here and there a child cried, only to be silenced by its mother. Geoffry could feel the weight of a thousand eyes resting on him.

Mounts had been saddled hours earlier and provisions packed in saddlebags. Now that their destination was known, there was nothing left to do but leave. Ordinarily so confident in his every action, Geoffry of Glencoe hesitated, reluctant to leave his home, his wife, his child, and all that were so dear to him. Though he could not see it, he knew that the Mistwall hovered blacker than the very night itself, a tangible presence just beyond the horizon. How did he dare to leave those he loved, knowing that he might never again see them again?

Moorlock's horse, an immense black stallion with wild eyes, pranced alongside, his iron-shod hooves clattering on the cobblestones, throwing up showers of sparks, and the young prince reined him in impatiently. But still Geoffry hesitated. Alison stepped forward and raised their infant for him to kiss. Geoffry inhaled the sweet, milky scent of the child as he grazed her forehead with his lips. His eyes met those of his wife's, and he nodded once before he turned his horse toward the gate, his heart filled with bold resolve.

Cries and huzzahs broke out on all sides as soldiers and villagers alike cheered, not really knowing or caring what was going on. Geoffry raised a thin, pale hand in acknowledgment, while Moorlock rose high in his stirrups accepting the accolades. Although the crowd didn't know it, their king and his companions were off to save the lives and the future of this land. Moorlock and Geoffry, accompanied by two soldiers, passed through the gates and rode out into the night.

CHAPTER
4
Strange Doings

The day remained cold and damp and grey, with the sun hiding itself from sight behind masses of dark, brooding clouds. The wind blew briskly from out of the northeast, bringing with it the promise of a long hard winter. The rats on the wagon huddled together for warmth, but the travelers' cloaks did little to hold back the chill. The road had narrowed, so that Cal, Bith, and Hathor had to lead their mounts behind the wagon and bring up the rear.

The team of six horses pulled the wagon along at a brisk pace, but even so, they seemed to be making little progress toward the crossroads that led to the caves. Purkins looked again at a crumpled map he had been given, and handed it to Endril.

"See, it shows the crossroads just three leagues beyond Roanwood. There's a little creek, some trees, and an old cairn to mark the trail."

Endril squinted at the map. "If this bit of paper is an accurate representation. However, if we do not find a landmark soon, I shall get back on my horse and ride ahead for a look-see."

Shortly thereafter, a solitary babushkaed granny, bent low beneath a heavy bundle strapped to her back, passed them by without a glance. A goose, only its head snaking free of the sack, fixed its beady malevolent eyes on them, squawking and blatting rude goose jeers until the old woman lengthened the distance between them and was gone.

The rats were beside themselves leaping up and down on the bed of grain and hollering rat curses after the goose, casting serious doubts as to the legitimacy of its heritage, defying it to come back and fight. One rat was even so bold as to leap from the wagon, first to Cal's horse, then back to the mount carrying Bith. It then climbed up the back of the girl's cloak and perched atop her head shaking its little rat fist and screaming taunts of its own at the departing goose.

Bith had managed to endure the presence of the rats by keeping a good distance between herself and the wagon. Even if they were her rescuers, she had an abiding fear of the creatures and still harbored a deep dislike for them. Ripping her cloak from her shoulders, she stood up in the saddle and began to beat at her head, dislodging her neatly combed black hair as well as the rat, who flung out its little paws to save itself, caught a lock of hair, and hung directly in front of Bith's face, the two of them staring directly into each other's eyes. Bith began to scream. Terrified, the rat let go, bounced off her bosom, tumbled to the ground, and bounded back into the wagon in two great leaps, where it burrowed back into the pile of grain, seeking the safety of its companions.

Blackie, the talking rat, crawled cautiously on to Purkins' shoulder and commented quietly into the driver's ear, "Sheesh, did ya ever look into her eyes real close? I mean to tell ya, it's scary!"

Bith settled back down in her saddle and pulled her cloak back around her shoulders, struggling to regain her composure. "I don't want r-r-rats standing on my head! I'm tired and I'm cold and I'm hungry again too. And why aren't we moving? And, and, how can that old cow in the field over there walk faster than a six-horse team?"

Hathor, Endril, Purkins, and Cal stared at each other uneasily. The same worrisome question had occurred to each of them. The road passed beneath the horse's hooves, the scene seemed to change, yet they had not come to the little creek or the cairn mentioned on Purkins' map . . . And the farmer's field to the right . . . hadn't it been there for the longest time?

"That tree. It stay in same place long time," Hathor said, pointing to a distinctive, lightning-torn pine on the near horizon. And with a sinking heart, Endril realized that it was so. Just then, a powerful draft of freezing wind swept upward from beneath the wagon, flinging dust in the horses' eyes and causing their tails and manes to rise straight up. Cloaks and blankets were all but dragged from their owners' shoulders, and the rats hung on for dear life as a good third of the grain was blown off the wagon, exposing a few of the gold bars underneath.

And then the strange wind was gone as quickly as it had come, and in the silence that followed, there was heard a low chuckle. The four companions and Purkins exchanged glances. Bith groaned and hung her head. Endril leaned back against the seat and sighed dispiritedly. Hathor jumped down from his horse to the ground and began stalking around peering under the wagon bed, poking around in the grain and even looking beneath the horses' bellies.

"You won't find him there," Cal said in disgust. "You can quit looking. Come on out, Gunnar Greybeard. We know it's you."

"Gunnar Greybeard?" asked Purkins, turning to Endril. "Issat that dwarf we drank with under the tower that night?"

"The same," Endril said blackly.

"He's the one who keeps getting us into all this trouble," cried Bith. "Show yourself, Gunnar, you coward! You villain! Show yourself, so that I may kill you!"

"Now why would you want to do that, Elizebith, my

dear?" asked a soft, gentle voice which seemed to emanate from a point just off to Bith's right. Slowly, the air began to solidify, seeming little more than a bit of mist at first. It soon thickened, took form, and standing there on a mound of grass was a tiny old man smoking a briar pipe. He appeared to be no more than a sweet, harmless old grandfather whose worst offense might be the telling of a too scary bedtime story. But looks could be and often were deceiving, for the kindly old gent was not the dwarf Gunnar Greybeard!

"Just who in blazes are you?" demanded Bith.

Cal dismounted silently, circled round the wagon, and strode purposefully toward the old man, drawing his sword from his sheath with the harsh clang of steel. The look in his eyes revealed his intent, even as he raised his sword for a blow which would have separated the old man's head from his shoulders.

"Well, Caltus, I see you are still making do with ordinary, inferior swords," the old man said as he took the pipe from his mouth and gestured, without looking, at the shining blade, seemingly unaware of his imminent danger. The sword crashed down, flashing through the air, missing him by a hair, and buried itself in the ground. Furious, Cal heaved and tugged and pulled with all his might till his muscles bulged and his face turned crimson with the effort, but he could not free his sword from the earth.

"Now, now, calm yourself," said the old man as he turned and patted Cal on the back, much as one would pacify a small child having a temper tantrum. "And you, Bith, you look as puffed up as a stuffed goose.

"You have met me before, my friends, just never in this form. And for that, I am most grateful. I grant you, we've had our differences in the past and there have been a few problems I did not forsee, but surely nothing that old acquaintances such as we cannot overcome.

"Come here and join me, all of you. You too, Purkins, and your little rat friends if you wish. I have a plan to propose that may be of interest to you."

Ignoring their various exclamations of rage and dismay, the little old man waved his pipestem over the ground alongside the road, and instantly there appeared a roaring fire ringed with large stones. Suspended above the fire was a spit which turned magically of its own accord, and on the spit were a roast of beef, two hares, and four chickens, all nicely browned and filling the air with their rich aroma. Spread out before the fire on the chill ground were thick, woolly blankets, blue and red in color and covered with a multitude of plates and baskets heaped with steaming vegetables, baked breads, pickles, fruits, sweetmeats, and for the troll, a mound of succulent roots and tubers. There was even a pile of honeyed oats for the rats and several clay jugs of water. A large green glass bottle to the side of the blanket offered the promise of strong drink.

It was more than the troll could bear. "Hathor eat now, kill old man later," he said, trundling toward the blanket, followed by a wide-eyed Purkins and a horde of rats.

"No, wait, you don't understand, it's a trap," cried Bith as she held out her hands trying to stop Hathor, Purkins, and even the rats from leaving the wagon, but she might just as easily have attempted to stop rats from leaving a sinking ship, for lured by the promise of warmth, food, and drink, they paid her no mind.

"It's a trick. It's not real! The food will disappear; it's just magic!" she warned. But Purkins slid a roast chicken off the spit and juggled it from hand to hand. As he bit into it, the crisp skin crackled beneath his teeth and the juice trickled down his chin and his eyes closed with pleasure. Beside him, Hathor held two fistfuls of the raw roots, which crunched very realistically as he stuffed them into his mouth.

"I'm sure . . . it's a . . . trick," Bith said uncertainly as she slid down from her saddle and walked over to the blankets. She fingered the thick, heavy wool and imagined its weight covering her at night. She picked up golden fruit of some unknown variety and, almost against her will, brought it to her mouth. It was sweeter and more delicious than anything she had ever tasted. Bith sank to the blanket.

Endril, who still sat on the wagon with his arms crossed, sighed as Caltus gave up on his sword, and plucking the roast of beef from the spit, began tearing at the meat as though it had been months since he had last eaten a decent meal, in spite of the fact that the four had been eating like kings at the home of Lord Rotherham.

Endril left the wagon reluctantly and walked over to the old man. He leaned on his staff and looked down on him. He seemed so harmless, so small, yet all too familiar. "All right, Vili. What is it that you want of us this time?"

"Ah, Endril, you have seen through my little disguise," the old man said with a chuckle.

Bith's jaw dropped at the realization. Those eyes, that beard! It did indeed appear to be the god Vili, the little known brother of Odin, who had first brought the four together so long ago. It was Vili who had forged the runeswords and instilled them with his power, and it had been Vili who had sent the four from one end of the world to the other, seeking out and ultimately destroying those same swords.

The old man, his eyes twinkling in the best grandfatherly fashion, spoke again. "Tut! Tut! You all have such suspicious minds. Is it not possible for old friends to meet and eat together, to lift a glass of spirits without being accused of trickery and hidden plots?"

"If you are truly Vili," demanded Bith with her hands on her hips, "why have you come to us in this form? Why not demand that we bow to the . . . the . . . What was it you called yourself?"

"The Exalted Master? Ruler of the Twelve Spheres!" said Endril sarcastically. "Why the informality? Why the guise of an old grandfather?"

"Good questions; and I shall answer them." The old man indicated seats for all, and the group, including Endril, settled down around the cheerful fire, still filled with suspicions. "As you know," began the old man, "I put so much

of myself into those runeswords that I was thereafter unable
to manifest myself properly on your plane of existence, that
is, your world." He tapped some ashes out of his pipe and
refilled it from a small pouch. "I came to you in little pools
of water, or on the blade of a sword, or even in your dreams.
But all that is history now. Eat, drink, be merry! Let me
provide comfort for you all!"

"You forget who you're talking to, Vili," Bith spat out
angrily. "We know you, remember? Or have you forgotten
the matter of the many runeswords which we have sought
and retrieved for you and the trouble they brought us? That
last little mission nearly cost Endril his life. And of the
swords, well, as you yourself have noted, Cal is still using
an ordinary blade because the runeswords have a nasty habit
of melting away once they have served your purpose."

A pained look crossed the old man's face. "Making the
swords was a mistake, I'll admit that much. Ahhh, but they
achieved wondrous deeds in their time," he said, laying the
pipestem alongside his nose. "It was rash of me. . . . I was
trying to make a name for myself and I got carried away.
But time has passed, and I have learned from the experience. Yes, even we gods learn from our mistakes. Because
the four of you have destroyed so many runeswords, I have
regained much of my lost power. I am grateful for that, so
grateful that I no longer require obeisance from my most
faithful of servants."

"Well it's about time," said Bith.

"Still, you must admit you had fine adventures, and have
achieved wealth and fame beyond your wildest dreams. And
as for the swords melting away, well, I couldn't tell you in
advance, or you wouldn't have gone after them!"

"We could all have been killed, many times over!" protested Bith.

"Are you not all here? And very much alive? Have I
not watched over your every move? What purpose would
it serve if you were killed? I would be truly sorry if you
perished."

"Ha!" exclaimed Hathor as he grabbed another bundle of roots and a handful of tasty corms. "You find new suckers now, huh?"

The old man's eyes filled with tears which trickled down his withered cheeks. In spite of herself, Bith was moved. He looked so pathetic and alone and so very, very old. How was it that she had never noticed how old he was before? And how much he looked like her grandfather—in fact they might have been brothers. "You hate me," whispered the old man, his chin resting on his chest, shoulders bowed.

"It's not that we hate you," Bith said as she moved to his side and put her arm around the aged figure. "It's just . . . you've nearly killed us several times, and what have we gotten out of it? Nothing real at all!"

"I'm sorry," sniffled the old man, rubbing at his eyes with the back of his fists. "I never meant . . . but I understand. I'll just leave you alone now. Keep the food and the blankets. Perhaps they will make up in some small way for the trouble I've caused you. Just forget about the sword."

The old man rose to his feet, disconsolate, and began to walk off into the muddy field, his words disjointed and broken.

"*What*? What sword?" growled Cal, rising to his feet, the remains of the roast still clenched in his fist.

"Oh, nothing, just another runesword. Quite close, actually, but never mind. After all the trouble I've caused you, I couldn't . . . I wouldn't dare ask. . . . Besides, it will just melt away in the end!"

"WHAT SWORD?" roared Cal, closing the distance and placing himself directly in the old man's path. "Another runesword? Where is it? Tell me!"

"But, Bith and Endril said . . ."

"Never mind," Cal interrupted with a singleness of purpose. "We four expect to take chances, risk our lives. It is my destiny to possess these runeswords. . . . Tell me what you know!"

"Well, if you insist," Vili said in a small voice. "Through

means which I will not mention, I have learned the where-abouts of another of my runeswords. Best of all, it is quite near and may be attained easily without danger or difficulty. Perhaps, if you have nothing better to do, you might wish to acquire it."

"If it's so close and easily had, why don't you just go get it yourself?" Cal asked suspiciously. "Why? Tell me."

"As you can see, I can manifest myself only as an old man, Caltus Taliensen. I do not have the strength it takes to win such a powerful sword, or to destroy it. Such a sword belongs in the hands of one such as yourself, who will use it for right and not merely for might."

"You have many manifestations, Vili," Endril said dryly. "You have merely chosen this form to win our sympathy. Had you appeared in another form, less pitiable, we would not even have listened to your words, but would have cut you down for the lying scoundrel you are."

"Cut me and I bleed," replied Vili, taking a dagger from his belt and slicing his finger as he spoke. A drop of bright crimson blood appeared. "Alternate images are thin layers of unreality. They have neither blood nor bones; they cannot bleed. This is the one true face of Vili."

Endril sighed. He looked at his companions and saw the same look of resignation and sense of inevitability that he himself was feeling. Could it be that Vili was actually telling the truth? "Tell us, Vili. Tell us what it is that you want us to do."

CHAPTER
5
Magic and Mercenaries

The old man, on hearing Endril's request, smiled glee-fully to himself. Then, wiping his joy from his face, he turned and walked back to the camp without a word. For the rest of the afternoon, Purkins, the rats, Endril, Cal, Hathor, and Bith sat round the fire with the old man, enjoying the warmth and the feast. Much to Bith's sur-prise and great pleasure, neither the food, the drink, nor the fire proved false. Her initial suspicions melted away with each sip of the wine, which had to have been made from grapes of a glorious vintage and imparted all the silky warmth of a glorious and sensuous summer's day. The fire was real as well, despite the fact that the smoke rose straight into the windy sky without blowing into their eyes or throwing embers onto the woolly blankets. Nor was there a need to search for firewood, as the flames did not consume the logs and the fire showed no sign of diminishing.

Vili remained an old man, his features never blurring around the edges as false reincarnations were wont to do, and Bith was forced to accept that the man was really what he appeared to be, or that he was very, very good. Or perhaps both. He enchanted them with stories, filling their heads with grand visions of heroes and heroines, treacherous villains and hideous monsters. Of lies and deceits and treacheries untold. Of love and honor and unflagging devotion.

At long last the old man's story became dead serious as he spoke of the struggle between good and evil, and how the Dark Lord sought, with the aid of the giants, to overthrow the true gods and take their bright abode in the sky and turn it into a bleak and dismal hell. This bit of information seemed to bring the celebration to a close. Cal was pleased to discover that the battle with the Dark Lord was being fought in the land of the gods as well in his own gloomy world.

The night was cold and clear and the stars glittered like crystals strewn across the dark sky. The fire crackled sharply and the spit once again hung heavy with roasting meats, although none of them had seen how or when it had been done. They blinked their eyes and shook themselves back to alertness.

"But now to business," said Vili, filling his pipe from a leather pouch and lighting it with a brand from the fire. "Let us speak of the sword."

"Yes, the sword," agreed Cal with enthusiasm.

"You will not have to cross oceans to find this sword," said the old man, "for it lies yonder, buried beneath those hills." He gestured into the blackness of night behind him.

"Now, why exactly, is it you can't go fer this sword yerself?" came a tiny voice by the fire. It was the rat Blackie, his red eyes glowing in the light of the flames, staring a bit suspiciously at the old man. "Why d'ya need our frens here ta do yer work?"

The old man glared at the rat from under lowered brows. "I do not make it a habit of speaking to lesser creatures," he replied tersely, "but in case you were not listening earlier, there are other forces at work here, and until more of my power returns, these four, my true and loyal servants, must serve me once again."

"Just askin'," Blackie said in an innocent voice, and then quickly became very interested in coiling his tail around his paw.

"Hrmmph!" growled the old man as he stroked his beard angrily. "And there is magic involved too. No one magic-user, no matter how powerful, knows everything. There are many layers of magic wrapped around this world. Some of it is specific, laid down with but a single purpose in mind; others are more broad in their intent and involve many complicated aspects." His listeners, especially Bith, grew quiet and drew close, for seldom did a powerful magician, let alone a god, deign to explain how things worked.

"Think of spells as fences," instructed the old man. "The spell that hides the sword from us was like a fence that shut out sight, sound, and even emanations of the sword's existence. But that spell could easily have been enclosed by yet another spell that covered the sword's aura as well as everything else around it. The Mistwall itself is such a spell. Now, some of the power that went into hiding the sword has been used in an attempt to shield it from the Dark Lord's power. That weakness, that lowering of its defenses, has permitted me to find it. But I fear that if you do not acquire it quickly, the Dark Lord will. Speed is of the essence."

"Well, let's go!" cried Blackie, leaping to the top of Purkins' head. "Time's a wastin'!"

"That will not do!" said the old man sharply. "A wagon laden with a load of rats, grain, and gold will not be able to go where the sword may be found. Besides, I believe you already have a mission of sorts?

"*You*," he added pointedly, singling out Blackie with a hostile glance, "should continue on with your master to the ogre caves."

"But, sir, what if they need our help?" Purkins asked softly, twisting his cap in his big callused hands.

"Thank you for your concern, Purkins," Endril said, turning to the man who had shared his dungeon cell. "But we will be all right, and after all, you have a cave full of ogres to worry about, not to mention your wagonload of furry friends."

"But the cave is not far from here," Purkins said, brightening. "We can deliver our goods and then help you to find this magic sword. The rats and I make quite a team. They go with me everywhere. What I do, they do too. I be a man of my word."

"It's clear you do not have a wife," Bith muttered under her breath.

The old man frowned but said nothing.

Endril looked at the others, but Hathor had stretched out on the soft blanket, and his beard fluttered with the strength of his snores. Cal waved a hand indifferently and Bith only shuddered. Endril smiled down at Blackie and then turned to Purkins. "It would appear that we are officially joined in this enterprise."

"Now that the rat issue is settled, can you tell us more about where we will find this sword, or is that a secret?" Cal asked impatiently.

"And can we use it to stop the Mistwall once again, as we did at Cairngorm?" added Bith.

"I can give you clear and precise directions on how to find the sword," replied the old man, "but I cannot say what you will be able to do with it once you have it in your possession. However, if it can be kept out of the hands of the Dark Lord, it certainly will not enhance his already considerable powers. That alone is reason enough for finding it."

"True," said Endril. "Well, come, Vili, share your knowledge so that we may begin our journey. Soonest begun, soonest done."

"You will find the sword in a cave high in the hills not more than a league east of Cairngorm, or at least what was once Cairngorm."

"Cairngorm! But the Mistwall has taken Cairngorm!" cried Bith. "You surely do not expect us to venture into that horrible darkness."

"The sword is, as yet, safe," said the old man. "If you are swift, there will be time."

Bith stared at the man suspiciously, wondering how it was that he seemed so certain. Did the Dark Lord consult with him or share his timetable of destruction? But she held her tongue as well as her doubts.

There followed a lengthy description of streams bending this way and that, oddly shaped boulders, and leaning trees. A map was drawn in the coals with a stick. Bith and Purkins, however, soon lost track, but Endril and Cal followed the old man's every word, and when he was done they were able to repeat his directions without a single mistake. Even Blackie had it down pat! Bith smiled secretly. Maybe that rat would have his uses after all.

It was dawn when they finished, and Endril and Cal set about packing the foodstuffs, which would come in handy for the journey. Bith made herself useful rolling the blankets into bedrolls, tying them securely and piling them on the wagon. Hathor snorted and wakened; then Cal filled the troll in on the plan. Dawn was brightening the horizon, when suddenly the fire vanished, and with it, the old man.

Purkins shook his head. "Very strange old fella, that guy!" Then he hitched up the six horses, and the wagon was ready. The four heroes mounted their horses, and the strange expedition took to the road once more, setting their course east, through the oncoming maelstrom that was the Mistwall, once more in search of a runesword.

Geoffry and Moorlock and the two soldiers rode slowly through the cold, moonless night, their horses sensing rather than seeing the roads that they followed. Soon, the cold bit its way through their coats and cloaks, and all wished they had dressed more warmly. One of the soldiers suggested

that they stop to make a fire, but Geoffry drove them
on, till at last they came to a crossroads with a large,
well-lighted inn.

The young king at last relented, and the shivering group
led their horses to the stable, following which the men
repaired to the warmth of the fireside. The hour was late,
and the innkeeper nearly threw them out. But then he
recognized the King of Glencoe and started to call out
the servants.

"Do not arouse the house, kind sir," whispered Geoffry,
"for our journey is most secret. If we might just have
some brandy to warm our insides . . ." The innkeeper nodded and hurried off to the kitchen to honor the king's
request.

"If this be Quixham," said Moorlock, unrolling a map
from within his coat, and spreading it out on the table, "then
we've covered two leagues so far, my lord."

Geoffry frowned. "We'll have to do better than that if
we are to overtake the four by tonight!"

"We'll travel faster by day, of course, and we can catch
the byroad here for Roanwood." Moorlock traced their
course on the map, while the king and the two soldiers
looked on. Then the innkeeper returned with the drinks,
and the cold travelers warmed themselves with the brandy.
Soon the account was settled and the men set out once more
on their lonesome journey.

"Where's my gold?" demanded Gorvorn, smashing his
meaty paw down on the rough hewn table. "I don' need dis
stinkin' parchment!" A tin cup fell to the rock floor with a
clatter.

Purkins winced. He had never dealt with an ogre before,
and as far as he was concerned, he never would again, not
for any amount of gold. He explained one more time.

"Make your mark on this here paper, just there," he said,
pointing, "and you'll get your damn gold! My king wants
a signed document. . . ."

"Don' sign documens!" interrupted the snaggletoothed ogre, this time standing up in fit of rage. "Want my gold now! Word of Gorvorn good as document!"

Purkins winced as the ogre's breath caught him full in the face. Hathor, who was standing behind, nudged him and whispered, "Better get gold, forget paper!"

"Your word, then!" blurted Purkins. "I'll send for the gold!" Gorvorn, and the ogres behind him, broke out into what might have been construed by some to resemble smiles, and growled under their breath.

Soon, Cal and Endril tramped into the smoke-filled room with two heavy sacks which they tossed up onto the table with a heavy clank. Gorvorn's red eyes lit up and he ripped open a sack revealing the shiny gold bars within.

"This buy my soldiers!" snarled the chief ogre. "One moon! Only one moon!"

"Agreed," replied Purkins. "My king will send more soon!"

"Let's get out of here," Cal whispered, out the side of his mouth.

Several more ogres came lumbering out of some unlit side chambers, and a mad scramble began for the pile of loot on the table. Purkins and the others made their way silently out the way they had come, and were glad that no notice was taken of their departure.

Once out of the cave and back in the fresh air, Purkins breathed a sigh of relief. "Gawd, I'm glad that's over."

"How'd it go?" Asked Bith, who was waiting uneasily by the wagonload of rats.

"A piece of cake," replied Cal with a grin on his face, nudging Purkins with his elbow.

"It would seem King Ethelrud has bought himself some real tough allies!" said Endril with his usual sarcasm. The elf mounted his horse.

"No, seriously," insisted the girl. "Will they fight with us against the Dark Lord?"

"Not likely," replied Cal.

Purkins shook his head. "Honey, I wouldn't trust those ogres farther'n I could throw one of 'em with one hand!"

"What a waste of money!"

"Not quite," Said Purkins with a smile, holding up three gold bars in his hands. "I got my share! This'll buy a lot of grain!" The rats broke out into a chorus of squeaky cheers.

Hathor came shambling out of the cave. "Better go fast, ogres have big fight inside, may come!" The troll glanced over his shoulder into the cave. "Think we have more gold out here!"

Purkins face went white and he shoved his gold bars inside his vest.

"Let's be off! We have a runesword to gather!" proclaimed Cal. "It's still morning and we have a fair distance yet to travel!"

With that announcement, the others mounted up quickly, Purkins hopped onto his wagon and clucked at his team, and soon the procession was rolling back up the valley toward the main road.

CHAPTER
6
The Artifact

The journey to the cave described by the old man was not long but very tiring. Soon after leaving camp, they came to a bent tree and reluctantly took their leave of the east-west road. They made their way up a narrow rutted track that climbed steadily and steeply into the hills. Thanks to the old man's provisions, there was an abundance of food, which they shared with the occasional refugee when they stopped to eat. Also, Hathor had thought to capture some of the embers from the magic fire, inside an empty gourd. The embers never went out, no matter how long they were enclosed, and never failed to start a blaze no matter how wet the firewood.

And wet it was. The higher they climbed, the wetter it became. It was not an out-and-out downpour but a sullen, heavy sleet that leaked steadily from the dark skies, weighing down their spirits as well as their clothing. Twice during the day they were forced to stop, wring out their clothes, and dry them by the convenient and ever available, welcome fire.

As they gained altitude, the land quickly turned bleak

and hostile, almost as if it knew the Mistwall was soon to arrive. The track was filled with sharp-tipped briars and deep, murky bogs. They camped that night under the shelter of an overhanging rock, and all were extremely glad for the fire, which so far, had not failed them. Bith studied her new spellbook by firelight, and just before Hathor fell asleep, he was entertained by a group of large rocks, which the girl animated, giving them feet and legs. The dancing rocks frightened the rats, who scurried about in terror. Blackie and all his furry comrades were pleased when the stones finally settled into the ashes by the fireside.

The next morning, the sun, when it chose to rise, was weak and watery and soon hid its face in shame, sliding behind dark clouds as though grateful to escape. Of people, there were none, and although there were soft slitherings and shy rustlings in the underbrush, they saw no sign of game. The land rose steadily underfoot, a series of rough crags and steep gullies, climbing higher, always higher.

By noon, the track narrowed to a tiny gap between great rock spines, and the wagon would go no further. Endril and Cal conferred with Blackie and all agreed that they had found the second of Vili's guidepoints. It was an immense boulder, a stele of some sort, carved from base to pinnacle with strange glyphs which none of them could decipher. The stone leaned at an extreme angle and, with the cliff behind, formed a natural shelter in its lee.

In this obvious campsite, Purkins and the rats, in spite of their objections, were left behind to watch the wagon and all the horses, as even the mounts would be of no further use to their riders. Blackie, however, was adamant, and after several minutes of useless argument by Bith, the four heroes finally agreed to take him with them to the secret cave.

They departed the place on foot, using the stone as a directional sighting as they had been instructed. By nightfall they had climbed still higher and found the third marker, a sharp bend in an icy, swift-flowing stream. Here they made a second camp.

Bith, her legs unaccustomed to the strenuous climbing, collapsed atop a large boulder and cradled her head in her arms, too exhausted to even begin to search for firewood or carry out any of the usual camp chores. She was tired and wet, her sodden clothes clinging clammily to her body. Her hair was plastered to her head and draggled down her neck and shoulders. Her shoes were reduced to soggy lumps, next to useless in contending with the cold mud and sharp rocks. She did not know if she had the strength to go on. She was filled with despair, and without thought, she drifted off into an uneasy sleep.

All around her, Hathor, Cal, and Endril busied themselves, for each in his own way was very fond of the girl. She did not have to voice her concerns, for through the many adversities they had faced together, they had become a team. Speech was not necessary; they had come to sense one another's moods and interpret them correctly. They all knew that Bith was near the breaking point.

When she wakened, it was to the scent of fresh baked bread and roasting meats. What's more, she was warm and the rain was no longer beating down upon her head! Bith rose and looked around in amazement. Her companions had erected a makeshift lean-to above her, and in the center burned a cheerful fire.

"Careful, you'll bring the whole place down. Do you like it?" Cal asked shyly.

"Like, it? Why, I love it! Oh, thank you!" cried Bith and she hurled herself at Cal, meaning merely to hug him to express her gratitude, but somehow, their arms got all mixed up and her head bumped into his nose, rather hard. She raised her head to apologize, and then they were looking at each other, Cal's brown eyes looking into Bith's silver eyes. And it wasn't Cal looking at Bith, his companion, his friend. It was merely Cal, a young man, looking at a very beautiful young woman named Bith who happened to be in his arms with her mouth mere inches from his own. It was too much to resist.

"OOOooo, Ugh! Yer not gonna wanta kiss us all, are ya?" whined Blackie. "I mean it's not really all that big a deal; we just threw together a little hut and trapped some rabbits. Yer not gonna try to kiss us too, are yuh?"

"Verdamt, mousker," grumbled Hathor as he conked Blackie on the top of the head. "She don't be kissin' us."

Endril watched the two as they fit their bodies close against each other and sighed softly before their lips met once again. He was glad for them. It had been apparent for some time that something was happening between the two, but still, there was a knot of sadness in Endril's chest which felt like a lump of coal. He cleared his throat and then picked Blackie up and set him on his shoulder. "Come, little friend, I think it's time to look for more firewood."

"More firewood? Why? Are you nuts er somethin'? We got enough to keep us warm fer a week, what with the way it washes up here on the rocks! Oh, oh, yeah, I getcha! Come on, Hathor, let's go get some firewood!"

The romantic moment passed quickly, and Cal apologized profusely, saying it was merely his lost love, Yvaine, who he had seen in Elizebith's eyes. As might be imagined, Bith took immediate insult, and was soon storming around the camp, kicking things with vigor. Out went the fire and down came the lean-to in short order.

"What are we doing, wasting time here by the stream?" she yelled. "Lets get our rear ends in motion and get going." Cal earned nothing but dirty looks from the others.

The day was grey, and the Mistwall could be seen boiling just beyond the next hilltop they surmounted. But to most of the party, the weather and the Mistwall were minor difficulties compared to Bith's rage. The remainder of the trip was made in silence, and by midday they had found the cave wherein the runesword was to be found.

It was a very ordinary-looking cave, low and overhung with brambles and grass, set into the face of a shallow bank.

Had it not fit the old man's description precisely, they might well have passed it by.

Suddenly, Hathor growled and caught hold of Endril's arm. "Look," he rumbled, and nodded toward the dark opening in the hillside.

"What is it? What's the matter?" asked Bith, the anger of the morning forgotten.

"Something has been using this cave," said Cal. "Look, there's a clear path and trodden quite deep. Something uses the cave a lot." His hand moved to his sword just as Hathor and Endril reached for their weapons.

"Wait, couldn't it be an animal? You know, rabbits or something using it for a den?" Bith seized Cal's sword arm, with more than usual concern.

"Or wolves," added Blackie.

"No animal. Man," grunted Hathor, pointing at the muddy trail with a large and stubby dirt-grimed finger. Bith followed the dirty digit and saw, with sinking heart, footprints, undeniably those of a man.

Endril signaled silently, and Hathor and Cal circled around to the far side of the cave entrance. Endril took his place on the near side of the cave mouth and drew his sword without a sound.

"No need to pussyfoot around, sneakin' here an there like I be some sort of danger to the likes o' you," said a gruff voice, startling them all with the suddenness of the unexpected words. "But set one foot in my cave and yer all goners!"

"Who are you, friend or foe?" demanded Cal. "Show yourself!"

"And have you run me through with your swords? I think not," said the unseen speaker.

"Why would we do that?" asked Endril.

"How should I know? If you mean me no harm, why are there three of you armed to the teeth standing outside my home demanding that I come out? Just go away and leave me in peace."

"Good sir, we mean you no harm," said Endril sheathing his sword and stepping directly in front of the cave so that its hidden occupant might see him clearly, making certain that his hands were kept well away from his blade.

An uneasy grumble issued from within.

"We have been sent to this place to find an artifact," continued the elf. "An artifact which we are told is to be found in this very cave. Do you have knowledge of such a thing?"

"And if I did, why should I tell you?" came the surly reply. "If there is such a thing in my cave, then it must belong to me!"

These words caused great consternation among the heroes, and had Endril not hurried to Cal's side and spoken with some urgency, Cal might well have dashed into the cave to do battle with the still invisible speaker.

"If it is yours, sir, then tell us what it is." Endril said, returning cautiously to the mouth of the cave.

"If it is mine, then I must know what it is already. Therefore, *you* must tell *me* what you think this artifact to be."

"It'll be my blade up your nose if you don't stop playing games and come out of there!" Cal roared as Hathor clung steadfastly to his arm, holding the boy back.

Back and forth the arguments flew, but neither side was able to claim the advantage. The inhabitant of the cave stubbornly refused to either show himself, come out of the cave, or admit that the "artifact" existed. The heroes also refused to leave or tell the cave dweller just what the artifact was. Nor could they go in and drag him out, for he had the clear advantage. It was his cave. The gods only knew what sort of traps he had rigged against an invasion. Despite their determination, they could not take the risk of finding out.

Bith was rummaging through her belt of magic accoutrements, ready to cast a spell of charm, when Blackie came up with the solution. "Waddya say we grease 'em?"

"Beg pardon?" said Endril.

"Ya know, grease 'em wit somethin' he wants. Make it worth 'is while!"

"Oh, a bribe," said Endril, stroking his chin and pondering the rat's advice. "Not a bad thought, but what do we have that would be worth his interest? We've nothing of value to offer."

"Geez, listen up, bub. Dis guy lives in a cave, a zillion leagues from anywhere. I don' even wanna think what he eats. I bet everything we got would look good to him, an' what about some o' that troll's magic fire!"

"He's right," Bith said, frowning down at the rat. "Much as I hate to admit it, he's right. Come on, everyone, empty out your pouches and pockets. Lets's see what we've got that would interest this creature."

The group hastily retired to a small clump of trees, where they heaped their possessions atop one of the blankets. When they were done, there were four sharp knives, six flints and four striking stones, two flasks of oil, several vials of healing unguent, two combs, a long silver necklace with amber beads, a small silver-backed mirror, an assortment of mugs and dishes, the bottle of wine, some dried fruit, two handfuls of cracked nuts, a linty stuck-together lump of licorice, a silver whistle, half a smoked rabbit, two blankets, a small figure of a squirrel cleverly carved from a twisty bit of root, and, of course, Hathor's gourd with the magic embers within.

Carrying the blanket between them, they returned to the clearing and spread their booty on the ground in what they hoped was an attractive fashion. Bith's sharp ears caught the sounds of movement at the mouth of the cave, but the shadows were too dark to detect the hermit.

"Hello, in the cave," Bith said in her most winning tone. "We are willing to trade for the information that we seek. Here, before you, are all that we possess. Take what you will in return for the answers to our questions and access to your cave."

Bith could feel the creature standing at the dark entrance—all her senses told her so, yet there was no reply. "We have nothing else to offer, save violence, and we wish you no harm. Will you not accept our offer?"

"What can I have?" came the reply. A hint of slyness had crept into the tone.

"What do you wish?" asked Bith.

A scraggly bearded man, only half-clothed in a dirty, matted fur, emerged from the cave. Obviously a hermit.

"Gimme everything," came the answer. "I want it all, and the blanket too."

There was a cry of dismay from Cal, and a harsh grunt from Hathor. Bith looked back at the others, uncertain what to do. None of them had even considered the possibility that the hermit might demand everything.

"You cannot have all of the knives," said Cal. "You may have one, but not all."

"Not licorice," muttered Hathor.

The haggling began, and continued for some time as each of the heroes struggled to protect some silly personal prized possession. When it was finally done, it appeared that the hermit had gotten the best of the deal. They had been forced to relinquish everything, save the rest of the blankets, two of the knives, and one of the flints and strikers, to learn what they wanted to know and gain access to the cave. The hermit was unbending, and they felt fortunate to have won back the little they had.

At last, just as night was falling, the hermit scurried down from the safety of his cave and knotted the blanket around his hard-won booty. He was a queer little figure, human, but short—at best no more than four feet tall, bent and gnarled and dark, although whether from race or dirt, it was impossible to tell. Close up, his garments appeared to be a rough covering made of little more than leaves and grasses woven together. His feet were shod with sandals made of bark and his hair was long and coarse and hung to his waist. He stroked the soft blanket with nervous fingers and eyed the group suspiciously as though he thought they might try to take back his treasures.

"Be at rest, good sir, we will not harm you," Endril assured him, even though Hathor continued to growl and grumble ominously. "I am the elf Endril," he said, and then, gesturing in turn to each of his companions, he introduced them. "This is Elizebith . . . Caltus . . . Hathor . . . and our diminutive friend here is called Blackie. We have come a long way in quest of something that will help us to stop the evil black cloud that looms over the horizon. Pray tell us your name."

"Bramble's the name, an' I don't care about no black cloud. I lives in a cave!"

The elf continued. "And what you know of the sword that is hidden within your cave?"

"I know nothing," said the hermit. "Never saw any sword."

The four looked at each other, aghast.

"But you said . . . !" wailed Bith.

"Never said any such thing," replied Bramble. "You did. You was the ones claimed there's an artifact in here. I never said nothin' one way or th' other."

"Me cut him up!" roared Hathor, and this time it was Cal who clung to the troll's arm, holding him back.

"Wait!" cried Endril as the hermit began to edge away, holding the bundle tightly. "Is there anything you can tell us? Is there anything in the cave that we should know about?"

The hermit paused, clearly torn between holding his silence and telling what he knew. He looked down at the bulging blanket and it was easy to see the play of emotions that crossed his face.

"Well . . . there's somethin' there," he blurted impulsively. "But I don't know what it is."

"Why not?" asked Cal. "How can you know that something is there and not know what it is?"

"The Arthana keeps it for itself."

"The Arthana?" The heroes looked at one another, perplexed. "Who or what is an Arthana?"

"Don't know," came the cryptic response. "Lives in the back of the cave. It don't bother me none and I don't bother it. Can't say what it would do to you."

By now, Bramble had edged further and further away, and before they could stop him, he turned and ran back into the cave, disappearing into the darkness.

CHAPTER
7
The Hole and the Stone

A frosty grey morning greeted Geoffry and his companions as they turned onto the byroad that led to Roanwood. They were chilled to the bone, but none would complain so long as the young king led relentlessly on, seemingly indifferent to the cold. At length they came upon a group of refugees huddled around a large fire, and the travelers dismounted and warmed themselves as Moorlock asked questions. However, none of the miserable peasants gathered around the fire had seen anything to match the descriptions given. So even before the warmth of the flames had time to penetrate their numbed bones, Geoffry and company were back in the saddle, once more trotting north along the road.

They passed several more groups fleeing the Mistwall, and finally stopped a bent old woman carrying a noisy goose.

"Oh the rats!" she shrieked in horror. "I never in all my days saw the like. It was a wagonload of the ugliest rats . . . and they called my Gertie foul names, they did!"

"It's them!" Moorlock exclaimed excitedly.

The old woman began eyeing the fat packs slung from
the sides of the horses. "Here, you wouldn't have a bit 'o
food for a poor starving old granny, now?"

"Of course. Michael!" Geoffry motioned to one of the
soldiers, who pulled out a small sausage and handed it
to the woman. Her eyes widened with anticipation. Just
then the goose wriggled free, grabbed the sausage, and
ran honking loudly down the road. The old woman yelped
and hobbled after, yelling a string of curses that made the
men blush.

Geoffry smiled. "Well, we're not too far behind them
now!" Encouraged, the king, the prince, and the two soldiers mounted up once more, and rode north, into the cold
grey day.

Flint was struck to steel, sparks flew, and fire grew inside
the cave, casting flickering shadows around the entrance.
Bramble was obviously enjoying his new-gotten booty.
Outside, night had fallen with a sudden swiftness, and
now the wind returned with a vengeance, howling across
the barren face of the bleak hillside.

The heroes huddled together for warmth, drawing their
cloaks over their heads for added protection. But their
efforts were futile, for the cold, driving wind sliced through
their garments and chilled them to the bone.

Bith's teeth were chattering as she said, "D-d-d-do you
t-t-think he'll let us share his c-c-cave?"

Endril scurried to the mouth of the hermit's home and
asked the question, couching it in the most convincing
terms. He returned to the group. "No, He says it's his
cave and it wasn't part of the bargain."

"But we asked for access!" exclaimed Bith.

"We change bargain," Hathor growled in a menacing
manner.

"No," said Endril. "That would not be the honorable
thing to do. We gave him our word that we would not
harm him."

"B-but we n-n-never said anything about f-f-freezing outside," shivered Cal. "And he has to know that we intended to come in and look for the sword. S-s-so why don't we look for it now?"

"Fine with me," replied Endril. "But I was thinking he might have some tricks or traps set for intruders."

"I'll t-take care of t-that," said Bith, shivering, and she reached into her all-purpose belt for the components of a spell. As the girl chanted an incantation, the cold, shivering group crept toward the cave and waited for a word from her.

"It's safe," she said at last, after running her hands around the entrance. "There are no traps."

The group pressed in through the small opening, and startled the hermit as he sat warming the smoked rabbit above his fire. His eyes grew large and he clutched the split of rabbit to his breast, thinking that they meant to take it from him.

"Don't worry, Bramble," said Endril as he dusted off his knees and wiped some mud from his cloak. "We want no trouble. The night is cold and wet, and as we have no shelter and we gave you all our provisions, we have decided to begin our search for the artifact now."

The hermit's eyes grew even larger and he looked from one hero to the next, their huge bodies filling the small cave from wall to wall and roof to floor, with Cal's sword and Hathor's mighty axe so close to hand.

"But you can't do that! The Arthana will be angry! You gave your word you would not disturb it!" wailed Bramble.

"We did no such thing!" Bith said sharply as she flung her hair back from her face. "We told you why we had come and what we wanted. We came for the artifact and we intend to have it."

"You mustn't disturb it," whimpered Bramble. His face had gone pale, visible even in the dim firelight.

"You could at least tell us where to look!" demanded Bith as she glanced around the small room.

The hermit's mouth opened and shut, yet no sound emerged. His frightened eyes darted to the rear of the cave and before anyone realized what he was doing, he had scooped up all of his treasures inside his bundle of blankets and dashed straight through the entrance into the night.

The heroes looked at each other, perplexed, trying to understand what had happened.

"I have a feeling that the old codger knows more than he's told us," said Cal. "What do you suppose an Arthana can be? Has anyone heard of such a thing?"

No one, not even Blackie, had ever heard of an Arthana.

They warmed themselves for a moment in front of the fire, and though they were hungry, they were all anxious to get on with the search for the runesword. A quick search of the room revealed nothing. It was bare; the hermit had taken everything but the fire with him.

They looked at one another in the flickering light. "Soonest begun, soonest done, eh?" Endril said with a forced chuckle. "Come, my friends, it is time to find out about this Arthana."

"I'll wager *it* is guarding the runesword," said Bith with a sigh as, one after the other, the heroes fell into line and followed Endril to the back of the cave.

The cave was surprisingly shallow, the roof tapering down until they were all bent over, literally crawling on their hands and knees. The cave proper ended abruptly in a small, inky-black opening which seemed scarcely large enough for Bith, much less the rest of them.

"Why are you looking at me like that?" cried Bith, feeling the gaze of her companions resting on her. "Oh, no you don't! I'm not going in there by myself! Never! There could be horrible things like spiders and rats in there!"

"Hey!" Blackie squeaked indignantly.

"Say! That's it! You go, Blackie. You go in through that hole and tell us what's there!" Bith cried ecstatically, clapping her hands and looking at the rat with sudden favor.

The rat stood on its hind legs and began pulling nervously on its tail. "What! Go in dere all alone and face that, that arthany thing?" Blackie's shrill voice grew even more high-pitched at Bith's suggestion. "Uh-uh, not dis rat!" He quickly turned and made a dash for the entrance to the cave. But Bith was quicker still. Stepping on the end of his tail, she picked him up gingerly by that long, thin appendage and lifted him up so that she might look him in the face. As he dangled helplessly before her, she spoke in a voice that oozed sweetness.

"Blackie, dearest, I know we haven't been the best of friends up until now, and I know that I've never adequately thanked you for your courage in helping to rescue me from Murcroft's tower, but I always meant to. It's not every rat who would stop to help a girl in distress." Bith fluttered her lashes at the captive rat.

"I, uh, well, I . . . uh, it wasn't nothing," Blackie said modestly as he swung back and forth from Bith's fingertips. And even in the half-darkness, it could be seen that his ratly resolve was failing.

"I would so appreciate it," Bith continued, "if you would just scamper on down this tunnel and see what it is that we're up against. We'll be right here behind you." The girl put the rat down on the floor gently and stroked the back of his neck. "And perhaps you'll find some nice little rat buddies who can tell you where our sword is and how we can get it without meeting up with the Arthana. You're so small and quick, no monster could ever catch you. Blackie dearest, say you'll do this one little thing for me, please, please, please?"

Hathor groaned aloud to hear the flowery nonsense that flowed from the girl's lips, and even Cal and Endril were forced to look aside. They could hardly keep from laughing out loud, so unnatural was the tone from their Bith. Blackie, however, was totally captivated, and his eyes shone brightly as he clasped his little paws and looked up at Bith adoringly.

"Uh, yeah, sure, uh, no problem. I'll just skip down dat tunnel an' see what I can see, an' if I finds that Arthana thing, well, it just better get outta my way!"

"Thank you, Blackie dearest. I knew I could count on you," said Bith as she knelt low and blew him a kiss, which fell just short of the squirming rat. The rat made a sweeping bow and then dashed directly into the dark opening.

"Was that a magic spell, or what?" asked Cal with a smile.

"Shame on you, Bith," chastised Endril. "I hope you have not sent the poor creature to his death."

"Oh, pooh," Bith replied with a flounce. "He'll be just fine. Like as not he'll find more little rats and they'll tell him everything we need to know. I think it was quite clever of me." She shot an angry look at Endril. "Besides, you seemed quite willing to send me through that hole and to my death! Hmmph!"

The rat was gone for a long time, and the companions grew cramped and tired waiting for him. A worried expression settled on Bith's face as the minutes stretched on and Blackie did not return. Despite her quick words, she would have cared greatly if something dreadful happened to the rat, for his irreverent words and breezy manner appealed to her whether or not she was willing to admit it.

There was no point in lingering beside the dark tunnel, since there was nothing to see or hear, and after a time, the companions one by one returned to the fire—all save Endril. The elf sat silent and intent, listening at the mouth of the dark hole. The others, relaxed by the warmth and wearied by the events of the day, drifted into sleep.

Schlein wiped the sweat from his massive brow and strode forward along the steaming, smoke-filled passageway, glancing furtively from side to side. Through holes in the walls he could make out vast furnaces where molten rock spewed forth like fiery water into huge cauldrons. Only once before had he been summoned to this dread place, a massive basalt fortress carved by the fire giants from the side of a living volcano. On that occasion he had just been turned away from Cairngorm by the accursed four, led by Elizebith of Morea. He had not enjoyed the dressing-down he had received for that failure and he was not looking forward to whatever awaited him now.

The blond-haired, barrel-chested magician wondered just what he could have done to have received a personal summons from the Dark Lord. The attacks all along the Mistwall this fall had met with resounding success. Cairngorm was his, Hamm was reduced to ashes, the wall was on the move. . . . Could it have been that moment of hesitation he had experienced before he set fire to Cairnwald? Did the Dark Lord know his every innermost thought?

No! He shook his head. Not even a god like the Dark Lord would bother himself with such petty details. Schlein came to a glowing iron gate, guarded on either side by a pair of immense fire giants clad in rusty red armor. The uglier of the two snorted at the sight of the magician, and pulled open the red-hot door with his bare hand.

"Go in. You are expected," boomed the giant in a deep, guttural voice.

Schlein could feel the intense heat emanating from the red-hot iron door, and the hairs on the back of his neck tingled as he tried not to look down while he walked with great care across a narrow bridge which spanned a seemingly bottomless black chasm. The bridge led to a stone gate, carved in the shape of a boar's snout, guarded by a second pair of hostile fire giants. One of the giants growled something unintelligible at him, and a portcullis clanked noisily open. Schlein was ushered into a great, smoke-filled hall, dimly lit by torches and stinking heavily of sulphur. The only path led past cells filled with screaming men, elves, goblins, and other, nameless, creatures, all enduring various degrees of torture at the hands of the local giants.

I am a man who prides himself on his methods of inflicting pain, but the excesses of the Dark Lord make me look like a saint, Schlein thought to himself with a forced smile. At the far side of the torture hall, he ascended a long, wide, obsidian stair, at the top of which stood an ornately carved but empty throne. The magician stopped at the dais and waited.

Then a small door appeared in the solid rock wall behind the throne, and a tall, bald man in grey robes lurched through the opening, grimacing in pain as though something were holding his arms behind his back. Schlein suddenly felt THE presence all around him. His heart began to pound with fear and he broke out into a heavy sweat, tugging at the gold chains around his thick neck. A voice spoke within his mind.

We have a problem!

The balding man in grey robes screamed in agony. Suddenly his body twisted itself with a dreadful snapping of bones into an impossible knot and fell to the stone floor in a bloody heap. Schlein's eyes opened wide as he now recognized what was left of the man. It was Kaerlyn, lord of the Grey Marshes, one of his own trusted informants in the court of King Ethelrud.

Your toad has informed us of something that must be dealt with immediately! The voice in Schlein's mind shook the very fabric of his soul.

They have located the Stone of Time! Schlein fell to his knees in agony, as jets of pain shot through his mortal body.

Stop them!

Schlein writhed in pain.

Find it! Bring it to me!

The presence was gone as suddenly as it had arrived, and Schlein fell limp to the floor. Some time later he struggled up to a sitting position and pondered the remains of Kaerlyn, then addressed the mangled corpse: "I suppose it would be too much to expect you to tell *me* what you told *him!*"

The number one servant of the Dark Lord struggled uneasily to his feet and made his way slowly down the obsidian stair, past the screaming torture victims, through the gate, and out the way he had come.

CHAPTER
8
The Arthana

Endril had almost decided to try to wedge his own body through the hole, when his sensitive ears picked up the clicking of rat toes. A moment later, two little red eyes appeared in the darkness, and Blackie emerged safe and sound.

"Hiya, Endril. Anything new happen here?" The elf held out his arm and the rat hopped aboard.

"We were beginning to worry about you," whispered Endril as he walked back toward the fire.

Elizebith awoke at the sound of voices, and a smile brightened her face as she sat up. "The explorer returns. Did you find the runesword? Or the Arthana, whatever that is?"

Cal and Hathor wakened, as well, and Blackie described his rather uneventful trip. He had seen no sword and found no monster. All that was there was a long, winding tunnel filled with skeletons, and a strange metal object at the end.

"No sign of the sword! You searched everywhere?" asked Cal, disappointment showing in his voice.

Blackie was indignant, "Hey, listen, bub, I grew up in a cave, you know, and furthermore my official name back home is See-In-The-Dark, so nothin' escapes these beady little eyes o' mine!"

"Sorry," Cal replied sheepishly.

"What about that metal thing?" asked Endril. "Could you pick it up and bring it back to us?"

"Not likely! It musta weighed a ton, even to youse big guys."

"What about the skeletons?" asked the girl. "Were they just lying on the floor . . . ? And what were they skeletons of?"

Blackie scratched his head and wiggled his nose. "I think they wuz from all kinds a things; there was little ones and there was big ones—horses or somethin' like dat—an dere wuz men, leastways some wit two legs, some wit four legs, ya know. Oh! an' what wuz mighty peculiar—them skeletons wuz jus' standin' there wit' nuttin', nuttin' at all, holdin' 'em up."

Hathor shook his head and grunted.

"You're sure you saw nothing else?" Bith was puzzled.

"Naw, nuttin' . . . except maybe I oughta tell ya about that wall back there." The rat pointed at the wall in the back of the cave, the wall with the hole through which they could not pass.

"Yes," prompted Bith.

"Well it ain't there. Dis whole place is jus' one long cave!"

A look of shock crossed the faces of the others. Bith slapped herself on the forehead.

"I should have known," cried the girl. She fumbled in her belt of magic paraphernalia and pulled out two amber stones which she then rubbed gently together. In a moment Elizebith had dispelled whatever magic there was and the whole back wall of the cave began to shimmer and then disappeared from view. They found themselves staring down a long dark tunnel.

"It was a wall of illusion," she said, shaking her head. "When I checked for tricks and traps on the way in, I did not think to continue the spell once we had come inside."

Cal was already digging in the fire for some suitable sticks with which to make torches. "Come on, help me make some lights"—he turned to Endril with a grin— "Soonest begun, soonest done. Time's-a-wasting."

Hathor and Endril lent a hand, and with a little work the four fashioned some makeshift but effective torches to light their way. With Blackie on his shoulder, the elf led the way.

"I'll keep the spell working," whispered Bith, "just in case there are more false walls ahead."

They marched forward a few steps, and the tunnel began to slant down gently. The floor was covered with a fine black dust that clung to their shoes and muffled their footsteps. Soon the light from the fire at the mouth of the cave faded to a pinpoint in the distance, and only the four feeble torches illuminated the blackness around them. Several paces further, and Endril stopped short. There, standing unsupported in the blackness was one of the mysterious skeletons that Blackie had mentioned.

They approached it cautiously, and Hathor reached out to grab one of the bones. It wouldn't budge.

"Hmmm, big magic," said the stoic troll.

"Stronger than my dispell anyway," remarked Bith. "Isn't that thing too large to have been a horse?"

"If that was a horse," Cal whispered in awe, "it was bigger than any horse I've ever seen, even a war horse!"

Endril nodded in agreement. "That was no horse."

The group left the skeleton behind and pushed even deeper into the cave. They soon came upon several more sets of standing bones, one on either side of the tunnel. This time they appeared human in form, and once again, nothing any of them could do would dislodge even the tiniest part of a skeleton.

"Strange that there is no trace of clothing, fur, or armor," observed Cal.

"Big magic," repeated the troll.

Cal's torch went out, and they stopped for a moment while he fashioned another one from the bundle of sticks he had brought with him. On they went, through the silent tunnel, passing several more large skeletons, and some tiny ones on the floor, till at last they came to the end of the cave and found the metal object Blackie had described. It looked like two very large chamber pots bolted together, with strange little feet to hold it up.

Cal tried to pick it up, and found that the rat was right—whatever it was, it must have weighed a ton. While Bith and Caltus investigated the strange object, Hathor and Endril felt around the walls for any sign of a secret door or passageway.

"Is your dispell still working?" asked the elf, with a yawn. Unlike the others, he'd had no sleep.

"Yes, why do you ask?"

Caltus too, yawned openly, and shook his head.

"It . . . (yawn) . . . just seems that we have reached a dead . . . end," said Endril in a drowsy voice. The elf sat down and leaned against the wall.

Bith found some strange writing on the underside of the metal object and knelt down for a closer look. "Oh, look, here are some instructions . . . *When cleaning the autom-a-ton* . . . How strange! *Do not touch the main* . . . Cal, hold your torch closer, would you? I can't read this."

There was no answer.

Startled, Bith stood up abruptly and looked around her. All her companions had fallen fast asleep—Cal on the floor beside her, Endril against the wall with Blackie leaning on his shoulder, and Hathor, snoring loudly, standing up in the middle of the room.

"Good gracious me!" she exclaimed, and then pinched herself to make sure she was not getting sleepy, too. She wasn't, and some of her panic subsided. What should she do? Elizebith began to pace in a circle around the metal object, deep in thought. One by one, the torches started going out, and she stopped in her tracks. The panic returned. She was breathing hard and her heart was pounding in her throat.

"All right, we need light," she said to herself. "I can handle that! All I need is a light spell." She dug the ingredients out of one of her pouches and said the proper words. "Now, what to cast it upon?" She glanced about the room. Hathor's torch was about to fade. Without thinking, the girl reached out and touched the troll on the top of his head. Instantly, Hathor lit up like a bonfire, illuminating the scene. Bith looked at the glowing troll; there was a sad, totally innocent look on his face. He also continued to snore.

"Sorry about that, Thor, but I needed to see!"

She pulled out the spellbook given her by Lord Rotherham and began leafing through the pages. Maybe there was an incantation in here to counteract sleep. A small, ominous clank at her feet sent a chill up her spine. The metal thing trembled, ever so slightly, and then set up a tremendous racket—whining, clanking, rattling, and whirring . . . and, much to Bith's amazement, it began to walk across the room on its four peculiar hinged metal feet!

"Oh no!" Bith screamed. "You stop that, whatever you are!" The thing was walking straight toward Endril and Blackie.

A thin, metallic voice echoed around the tunnel:

"Do not disturb Arthana!"

The girl tried standing in its path, but a metal plate on one side opened up, and out popped a long shiny arm that ended in a strange hand with jointed fingers. It grabbed her firmly and pushed her to one side, then continued on its way, rattling and clanking as it walked. Bith thought back to the spell she had cast to animate rocks, and tried reading the reverse at the metal thing. No effect!

The thing reached the elf, and a different metal plate opened and out came another shiny arm with a sinister spike at the end. The spike touched Endril in the chest. There was a sizzle and hiss with a cloud of white smoke.

Elizebith shook her head in disbelief. Where the elf and
the rat had been, there was now a seated skeleton, with a
smaller one on its shoulder.

Bith let out an ear-piercing scream and jumped on top of
the metal device, riding it like a small horse, and struggling
with all her might to wrestle the spike from the shiny arm—
all to no avail. The other arm merely pushed her over sideways so that she found herself being dragged along in the
dust of the cave floor.

"Do not disturb Arthana!" droned the metallic voice.
Then the arm with the spike reached out again and con-
verted Cal to a lanky skeleton.

Bith let out a noise resembling the shrieking of a she-
dragon as the metal device turned in short jerks toward
Hathor. Struggling to regain her balance, the girl's fingers
brushed over some indentations on the underside of the
object. . . . Suddenly it stopped moving and fell silent.

For a moment, Bith lay motionless beside it in the dust,
panting breathlessly, beads of sweat matting her hair, tears
streaming down her cheek.

When she had calmed down somewhat, her eyes focused
on the side of the metal monster. There, scratched in the
letters of an archaic language she had learned in her youth,
were the words:

Archimago's Automatic Automaton

Followed by the instructions that she had started to read
earlier.

"It's a machine!" she exclaimed incredulously. Bith read
on in amazement, mumbling the words to herself as she
went. In was written in a flowery, stilted language, but was
clear enough for her to understand:

*If thou wouldst disconnect the miraculous machine from
the source of flux, thus rendering it temporarily inoperable,
place the third digit of the left hand upon the red lever and
depress gently. . . .* Bith looked under the machine; her left

hand was still touching a red knob.

She sat up and dusted herself off as best she could, surveying the scene. Only the glowing Hathor remained of her companions; the others were now reduced to their skeletal form. She had to do something—and fast.

Bith slapped the machine with her palm. If she could stop it, she could jolly well control this Automaton, perhaps even command it to bring her friends back. She smiled to herself—*if she could control it*—well, the possibilities seemed interesting. Bith lay back down and attempted to read more of the writings on the side of the machine, hoping to discover more of its secrets.

Her hopes faded quickly. Much of the writing had been obliterated by a large burn mark, and she could only guess what would happen if she tried any of the other levers or knobs underneath.

She sat up again and dug into one of the pouches on her belt, removing three small leaves from a tiny jar. These were the last she had, taken from the rare Sapiea plant, impossible to replace, but needed. The leaves were believed to impart wisdom when properly consumed. Bith crushed them in her palm, closed her eyes, and carefully licked up all the particles with her tongue. For a moment nothing happened; then an overwhelming calm rushed through her body, and she was filled with confidence. Bith knew she would make no mistake.

She reached under the Automaton and, without looking, pushed one of the knobs. The machine began to clank and whirr once again. It walked purposefully over to the skeleton that had been Cal and touched it with its spike. There was a small poof of blue smoke. When the smoke cleared, there sat Cal, shaking his head and mumbling something unintelligible. The machine walked over to Endril and repeated its actions. The elf stirred, and the rat tumbled down into his lap, complaining loudly. The machine walked over to the troll, nudged him back to wakefulness, then clanked back to Elizabeth, and fell silent.

"Oh, my aching head." Cal was rubbing his scalp, "What happened?

"Hey!" exclaimed Blackie. "Getta load of the troll; he's a regular bonfire!" The rat scrambled back up onto Endril's shoulder.

Hathor, suddenly aware of his condition, began stamping around, slapping himself on the shoulders. "Ooch! Ooh! Hathor on fire!"

"Fear not, Thor," Bith soothed, still half dazed from the Sapiea she had ingested. "I cast a light spell, and you are going to glow for a few minutes." The troll stopped dancing and stared uneasily at one of his glowing hands, which he twisted unbelieving before his eyes.

Bith, meanwhile, began fumbling underneath the metal device once more, oblivious to her companions.

"We've been asleep?" asked Endril as he climbed slowly to his feet and stretched. When Bith didn't answer, the elf walked unsteadily over to Cal and helped the boy stand up.

"What's she up to?" asked Cal, leaning on the elf for support. Just then, the Automaton began to clank and whirr again, and all save Bith began backing away anxiously. The machine reared up on two of its legs. One of the metal plates opened up, and out came a shiny arm which rose upward. As the tip of the arm reached the roof of the cave, there was a flash of blue light followed by a small explosion.

As the dust cleared, a metallic voice spoke from within the machine:

"Awaken . . . Arthana, you have visitors!"

"Hey, look, gang!" cried Blackie, leaping from Endril's shoulder to the floor, and scampering across the room. Cal rubbed his eyes in disbelief. They stood in the center of a neatly furnished room, with a clean stone floor and multicolored tapestries hanging here and there. On two of the walls there were bookshelves packed with leather-bound volumes; at one corner of the room stood a finely carved table topped with an ornate candelabrum, complete with seven lighted candles; and in another corner stood a plain wooden bed with a straw mattress.

Blackie scampered up to the foot of the bed. "Oh, oh, this don't look so good!" On the mattress lay the wrinkled remains of someone or something long dead.

Elizebith stood up, and as though in a trance, walked to the bed, leaned over the dead thing on the mattress, and touched it gently.

"This was Arthana," she said to no one in particular. Then straightening up, she circled the room slowly, and stopped before the bookshelves. Eyeing the volumes carefully she pulled out a small dusty tome and began to page through it.

"It's her diary," she said reverently. "Arthana was a sorceress of the tenth order, in the time of the invasion. . . ." As Elizebith read on, the others began poking around the room, looking under things, pulling out drawers, and peering behind shelves. Blackie found a bag of oats, which he promptly ripped open and ate till he couldn't walk, then crawled to the table and lay on his back, with all four paws in the air, beneath the candles.

"Lemme know if ya finds anything ta drink," said the rat. "I just woiked up a thirst! Phew!"

Hathor finally stopped glowing and rubbed his hands together with a gleeful look. Meanwhile, Endril and Cal pulled back each of the tapestries, searching for any concealed objects, doorways, or runeswords.

"The Automaton," read Bith, pointing at the metal thing in the center of the room, *"was a gift from my old friend Archimago, who taught me much of what I know. He made only three. Endowed with many powers, the device serves me best as a watchdog, yet is more faithful than a hound, and never requires food. . . ."*

"Yeah, yeah," groaned Blackie. "But can it get me a bottle of wine?"

Bith read on in silence, while the others, now aided by Hathor, left no stone, or corner, of the place unturned in their search for the sword.

"Damn! It just isn't here!" complained Cal.

"Here is the last entry." Bith commanded the attention of the others. *"I have been poisoned by the Dark One, and have no antidote. Arlanth, my faithful, has gone to seek help. The Automaton will guard me while I sleep. If Arlanth does not return . . . "*

"A sad story," said Cal, quietly. "I wonder if the Dark One is the same guy as this Dark Lord in charge of the Mistwall."

"The time of the invasion was over eight hundred years ago," said Endril, more to himself than to the others.

"Can you do anything for her, Bith?" asked Cal. "Maybe some kind of rejuvenation or something?" He looked uneasily at the twisted remains in the bed, and then turned his head from the awful vision.

"She's beyond my help." said Bith, putting down the diary. "We must give her a fitting burial."

"What? In here?"

"Don't be dense," said Bith. "Out in the valley by the stream."

"But what about the runesword?" the boy complained. "I won't leave without it."

"You wouldn't be leaving at all if it weren't for me!" Bith's tone of voice silenced the boy. "That Automaton turned you into a skeleton!"

Cal gulped.

"We must get out of here," continued Bith. "I think I can control the machine, so we'll take it with us, along with the remains of Arthana. Hathor, you and Endril wrap her up in that blanket." Bith put the diary in her belt, searched for a moment, and then pulled two more tomes from the shelf and tucked them into her dress.

Ever so carefully, the troll and the elf folded the blanket over the twisted thing that had once been a great sorceress, and then carefully they lifted it up. A gleam of light shone up from under the place Arthana had lain. Cal let out a yelp for joy and rushed over to the bed.

"It's here!" he proclaimed triumphantly. He reached into the straw and pulled out a magnificent sword. The hilt was jewel-encrusted; the blade fairly shimmered. So brightly had it been polished it seemed alive even in the dim light of the candles. And there were carvings, little runes, inscribed along one side of the blade.

Caltus danced around the room with the sword in his hands, heedless of the others, who quickly ducked as the boy flashed the fearsome blade in their direction. Finally, Cal made a series of whirling attacks on an invisible opponent and sank the blade deeply into the table with a heavy *thwack*, just inches from where Blackie lay. The rat flew off the table as though he had sprouted wings.

"Hey! Hey! Cut that out! I'm on your side, remember!"

Cal shook his head and pried the sword out of the table. "Sorry folks, I guess I got a little carried away."

"We've seen this before, Blackie," remarked Endril with a wry grin on his face. "It happens each time Cal finds one of these swords."

"Well, remind me not ta be around if it happens again. . . . I coulda lost a tail there!"

Cal pulled his old sword out of its sheath and tossed it on the floor with disdain, then carefully slid the runesword in its place. "I'm ready now. Let's be off"

Hathor took the blanket containing the remains of Arthana, Endril picked up Blackie from his hiding place under the table, and the companions stood in the center of the room, glancing uneasily at one another. There was one obvious question, and Blackie asked it.

"Hey, there's no door—how d'ya get outta here?"

The were surrounded on all sides by the unbroken walls of Arthana's room.

"I think I have the answer," said Bith as she knelt down by the Automaton and felt among the knobs and levers on its belly. "Endril, grab that candelabrum, so we'll have some light." The elf did as he was told.

"Now cover your eyes!"

Blackie climbed inside Endril's jacket and hid. Hathor closed his eyes, and again the machine began to rattle, clank, and whirr as it rose up on two legs and touched the ceiling with one of its arms. There was another bright blue flash and a cloud of dust and smoke. When it cleared, the companions found themselves once again at the end of the dark tunnel. All but one of the candles had blown out, so Endril quickly used that one to relight the others, and handed one to each of his companions. Then, with Bith and the clanking Automaton in the lead, Arthana's funeral procession began to make its way back out of the tunnel.

At length, they came to one of the skeletons they'd encountered on the way in, and Elizebith stopped and bade the machine revitalize it. A very startled young warrior, clad in chain mail stood before them in a daze. In a moment, his two servants and—much to Blackie's dismay—their three dogs were all brought back to life. Endril did his best to explain to the strangers what was going on, and the odd procession moved on up the tunnel.

The strange skeleton that was larger than a horse turned out to be a Carthean War Beast, a creature long since vanished from the land. It stood six feet tall, had a very mean disposition, and bore a nasty horn on the end of its nose. The beast, on awakening, began snorting and whirling, sending the dogs yelping and most of those in the tunnel scurrying one way or another for safety. Bith, however, cast the same spell she had used to calm the horses so that Hathor could ride, and the War Beast turned into an enormous, if potentially dangerous, pussycat.

Eventually, all were gathered back together, and they started on up the tunnel once more. On the way, Bith revitalized two more War Beasts, three thieves, and a holy man, all of whom had stumbled at one time or another into the cave, only to be trapped in time by the metallic hand of Arthana's diligent watchdog, the Automaton.

CHAPTER
9
The Procession

The forest of Roanwood disappeared behind the four horsemen as they urged their mounts into a steady trot. The cold drizzle which had soaked them all morning had stopped at last. As their dampened spirits rose, the pace increased.

They came to a small farm, and their leader drew them to the side. The shoulders of the road were deeply scarred with heavy wagon tracks. Nearby was a circle of stones, within which a fire had recently burned. Geoffry walked his steed slowly around the area while the others dismounted.

"This was their camp!" one of the soldiers declared triumphantly, as he poked his finger into the mud. "The ground is covered with the tracks of many rats. See them here, and under that tree."

"But was it last night, or the night before?" asked Moorlock, tugging absently at his dark mustache. He kicked an empty wine bottle into a puddle. "With all this rain and drizzle, it will be hard to tell."

"The fire's out cold," said the other soldier, who had been digging through the ashes with a stick.

"I'd venture to say we're two days behind them, then," said the king. "We must ride even faster!" He spurred his horse into action and splashed through a puddle back onto the road. The others hurried back into the saddle and followed as quickly as they could.

The displaced hermit, Bramble, paced nervously in the cold night air, wrapped in his new blanket, anxiously watching the entrance of his precious cave. Those fools were going make the Arthana angry, he just knew it. They would regret it. He had warned them. He told them not to go back there! A few minutes passed, and he toyed with the idea of sneaking back in, for he could see the welcome light of the fire he had started, flickering so invitingly through the narrow entrance.

Bramble crawled close enough for a peek inside, but was appalled to see the strangers sleeping around *his* fire. His heart sank, and he made his way back to one of his favorite hiding spots, where he tucked himself into the blankets as best he could and ate some of the delicious dried meat they had given him. Bramble would bide his time. By morning, he thought, the Arthana would turn them all to bones. Then old Bramble could reclaim his rightful home.

He leaned back, with his eyes set on the entrance, and half slept, oblivious to the cold, waiting impatiently for morning to come. Once, near dawn, he thought he heard a scream from inside. He sat up and peered at the entrance. The Arthana must be doing them in. Sort of a shame, he thought. This lot had been pretty nice to him, handing over all that food, the blankets, and the goods. Oh well! The world was full of fools. He had chosen to live here in isolation for that very reason.

The black sky was turning to hazy grey and the wind whistled through the scrubby pines. There would be no sunshine this morning. Two lone ravens flew over, cawing noisily at one another. Bramble watched the birds, and shifted uneasily in his crouch. He freed one hand so as to

flip the morning frost off his hair and out of his beard. Then
a familiar sound, one that he dreaded, made him fall deathly
still. It was the *clank clank* of the Arthana! Something was
terribly wrong.

There it was! Out the entrance of the cave waddled the
clanking Arthana monster. He was torn between curiosity
and fear. Was it coming after him? Bramble made ready to
flee, then stopped, not believing what he saw. Next out of
the cave behind the Arthana walked that pretty girl with the
dark hair from the night before, and then, one by one, her
companions followed. The hermit slapped himself on the
head in disbelief. Now there were other men coming out,
and dogs, and . . . and . . . the biggest things he had ever
seen, huge ugly horned monsters, snorting steamy plumes
of vapor in the cold air. He could feel the ground shake as
the beasts lumbered aimlessly in the clearing by the stream.

Bramble stood up cautiously for a better view. Now they
were having some kind of ceremony. Two of them had dug
a hole . . . and the girl was making a long speech full of
some fancy words. A burial. Somebody must have died. He
didn't care; he just wanted the whole lot of them to leave.
Bramble would just bide his time and then they would go.

The girl's words went on for some time; then her companions finally dropped something into the hole and covered it with a pile of rocks. Maybe now the whole lot
would leave, thought Bramble. Suddenly a mean growl
from behind sent a chill up his spine. Bramble jerked around
to see a pair of small black and white dogs, who began to
bark insanely, nearly frightening him out of his skin. The
hermit tried to shush the animals, but it was too late. The
girl saw him and called out.

"You up there, Bramble. Come down here. We won't
harm you. It is important that you come with us!" she
shouted.

"Go away and leave me be!" he snapped.

"Your cave will not be safe when the Mistwall comes!"
she persisted.

"Don't care about no wall." The hermit was now standing on top of a boulder, shaking a fist at the crowd below. "Go away! Git out! I've lived here a hunnert years, an' I'm gonna live here for a hunnert more!"

The girl was joined in her argument by the elf, but the two were unable to budge the determined hermit. It was his home and he intended to stay.

As the riders rounded the gentle curve, the sight ahead gave Moorlock pause for thought. Geoffry had seen it too, and both slowed their mounts to a walk. Large trees had been felled across the road, and a group of ogres was carrying another one on their shoulders. At a command, they heaved their load bodily onto the barricade with a crash, and then slapped each other on the back, pleased at their handiwork.

"What do you make of it, my lord?" Moorlock asked quietly. The four horsemen rode silently forward. "Should we not be avoiding these creatures?"

"Perhaps . . ." said Geoffry, deep in thought. He recalled sending a large amount of gold to . . . yes, that was it. "Perhaps these are the ogres with whom Ethelrud struck the bargain." His countenance brightened. "They must be!"

A horn sounded in the ogre camp and there was a small furor as several more ogres, armed with spiked clubs, rushed out of the bushes near the barricade. The tallest one advanced on the riders. He wore a tattered red sash around his chest, and a huge leather helmet covered his ugly head. In his gnarly hands he held a massive iron sword at the ready.

"Who are you? What are you doin' here?" demanded the tall ogre.

"I am Geoffry, King of Glencoe, liege of Ethelrud, King of the Westwoods, and these are my retainers." He eased his horse up to the ogre until they were almost eye to eye. "And you must be Govorn! We are allied against a common foe, the Dark Lord."

"For a moon!" grunted the ogre, hanging his sword back onto a buckler he wore under his sash. "Only for a moon." He waved the rest of his troops off. "Friends!" he said—and shaking his fist at the others—"Go back to work, you slugs!" The ogres with the spiked clubs grumbled among themselves and wandered off.

"The war will be won or lost in that amount of time, my friend!" Govorn had turned and was walking back to the barricade with Geoffry riding at his side. Moorlock was filled with doubts; what had the world come to that he should be allied with creatures such as this? But he and the two soldiers followed silently. Geoffry praised the ogre, admiring both his troops and the construction of the barricade. Moorlock smiled to himself. What use forty ogres and some fallen trees would be against ten thousand goblins, he could not quite imagine . . . but at least this band of ogres was fighting against the Dark Lord rather than for him.

When they asked about the four heroes, and the wagon of rats, Govorn let out a belly laugh.

"Heroes. Haw! Haw! Haw!" He slapped his knee. "There wuz a little boy with a sword, a smelly elf, a mud-sucking troll, and some girl, all uv 'em with the ratman, but no heroes!" Two other ogres, standing nearby, joined in the laughter.

Geoffry managed to draw out the fact that the ones he sought had left the ogre camp two days before, riding west toward the Mistwall. Govorn was quite sure they were all dead by now.

Without further ado, the king led his companions through a gap in the barricade and left the laughing ogres behind. Moorlock caught up with the king.

"What could they be doing now, my lord?" There was concern in his voice.

"Only the gods know. I only hope they haven't rashly ridden forward to do battle with the Dark Lord by themselves." The king, too, looked worried. "We need them to find the Stone . . ."

They rode on in silence for the next hour, and the advancing Mistwall loomed uncomfortably close, just ahead. They came to the bent tree where the wagon had left the road. The four examined the tracks at that point.

"They've gone up into this valley!" said Geoffry, relieved to discover that they would not have to ride straight into the Mistwall, as it had seemed. The riders abandoned the main road, and began the climb into the hills along the same rugged track that Purkins and the four had climbed earlier. All felt that they were close to their goal.

Geoffry pressed his men hard. Fortunately they were both loyal and made of stern stuff, quite used to enduring hardship. When darkness fell, they dismounted and traveled by torchlight, pausing at last to make a small fire and cook some food. The soldiers were fashioning more torches from rags when Moorlock, who had wandered off into the darkness, came running breathless back into camp.

"Take arms, the enemy!"

Hot on his heels were three drooling goblins, with swords drawn. Their large eyes glowed red in the firelight, and they were clad in black leather armor. The pursuers stopped short at the sight of Geoffry. In the firelight, his blond hair fairly glowed. He drew his two-handed sword and stood ready to strike. The king's soldiers dropped what they were doing, and unsheathed their blades as well. Moorlock rushed to his mount and unslung an axe from his saddle, then turned back just as four more goblins crashed out of the brush from the side.

Geoffry flew into action, his great sword whirling above his head like a deadly scythe. "Best smite them now!" he shouted. "There may well be more!" His blade lopped the head off the nearest goblin. The other two dropped their weapons, turned tail, and ran off into the darkness. The soldiers, meanwhile, had engaged the four attackers who had rushed in from the side. One of the goblins was already lying in a bloody heap near the fire, while the others backed warily away, parrying each attack.

Moorlock then let out a bloodcurdling yell and flew at the enemy with his battle-axe. The force of his blow split one monster clean in half. The king, now free, rushed at them from the other side. Both goblins dropped their short swords and turned to flee, but Moorlock's axe, then Geoffry's great sword, cleaved them into sundry parts. All fell silent. The fight was over almost as rapidly as it had begun.

"Is anyone hurt?" the king asked thickly. The four eyed one another, and all were well. "Good!" Geoffry picked up a rag and wiped the black blood from his gleaming blade. "Did you spy any more of those vermin?"

Moorlock glanced nervously around. "I think not, my lord. I was lying in wait and they fairly stumbled across me. I think it was just a scouting party."

"All the same we'd best move on." The king smiled. "I'm sure the Dark Lord has more willing servants wandering these hills tonight and they know we are here. Douse that fire and move out!"

The rest of their march went without incident, though the path was steep, and the going difficult in the meager light put out by their torches. Near midnight Geoffry and company gave Purkins quite a start, even though the rats had warned him, when the four cold and exhausted men walked up to his campfire, leading their horses behind them.

"We dare not stay here much longer," said Bith, perplexed at the stubbornness of the old hermit. "And I refuse to leave him here to face certain death."

"I'll tie him up, and Hathor and I can carry him down the hill!" suggested Cal.

Bith shot the boy a dirty look. Endril shook his head. "What about that machine?" He indicated the Automaton. "Do you intend to take it with you?"

Bith looked at the thing with a sigh. It held such powerful magic. But it moved almost as fast as a large tortoise. They would be days climbing down from the hills if it walked beside them. Sadly, she knew Endril had hit upon the answer, and shook her head.

"No, much as I would like to keep it. But it's too heavy to carry and too slow to keep up. We'll leave it behind, to guard the cave, and, possibly, protect Bramble from whatever comes with the Mistwall!"

She reached under the machine and pressed a sequence of buttons. The device turned and walked ponderously, and noisily, back into the cave. Bith then called to the half-naked man on the rocks above.

"You can go back to your cave now, Bramble. As you can see, I have returned the Arthana. It will protect you from harm!" Under her breath she whispered, "I hope!"

The recently rejuvenated warrior and his two servants scurried around the hillside gathering up the still barking dogs, while Cal and Hathor rounded up the wandering War Beasts and herded them in the right direction. Endril gave Hathor instructions to keep a special eye on the three thieves, and then the strange procession, with Bith in the lead, began its march back down the valley, following the trail by the stream.

Bramble, squatting suspiciously on the rocks, waited until the strangers were completely out of sight. He listened for a moment longer, then shouldered his blankets full of loot and hopped nimbly from one boulder to another down to the mouth of his cave and scurried inside.

The trip down the mountain was considerably more pleasant than the climb up. Most conveniently, the sun made a welcome rare appearance. The Carthean War Beasts, under Bith's influence, stayed docile, and fortunately were remarkably nimble for all their great size. The three thieves, under Hathor's watchful eye, remained sullen and silent, talking only among themselves in a strange tongue.

The rejuvenated warrior was called Philemus and he fell in with Cal. The two talked of many things as they climbed steadily down the hill. The man's dark face was half hidden by a thick black beard and his brown eyes were filled with a sad, faraway look. And well they should have been, for Philemus hailed from one of the Western Kingdoms, now under the thrall of the Dark Lord. The man, his dogs, and his servants had been trapped in Arthana's cave for over a hundred years, and he was greatly saddened to learn what had happened to his homeland in his absence.

Endril stayed close to Elizebith, keeping a close watch on her, as she was still behaving strangely and he did not know why. The elf had no way of knowing about the leaves she had taken to alter her perceptions. It was nearly sunset as they approached the rock spire under which Purkins had made his camp.

Geoffry and Moorlock stood on the path, with arms akimbo. Purkins waved cheerfully from behind. "See, I told you fellas you had nothing to worry about. I knew they'd come back safe and sound."

On seeing Purkins, Blackie hopped from Endril's shoulder and scampered back to his furry friends, eager to tell them of his brave new adventures.

The king brushed back his blond hair and smiled as he spoke to the newcomers. "You would be Elizebith of Morea." He reached out and took the girl's hand. "I am Geoffry, King of Glencoe"—Bith curtsied politely as he kissed her hand—"and I have been sent by my liege, Ethelrud, King of the Westwoods, to seek out you and your companions."

"We are most honored," said Bith humbly. She turned and introduced Endril, Hathor, and then Cal as he came walking down the path. The rest of the procession, including the War Beasts, marched unceremoniously around them as they spoke.

"And why, good king, have you sought us out?" asked Bith.

Geoffry winked at Moorlock. "It is known far and wide that the four of you can achieve the impossible!"

Hathor, Cal, and Endril glanced uneasily at one another.

"And that is what you would have us do?" asked Bith.

"Indeed, it would seem that the fate of our world is in your hands!"

Cal grabbed the hilt of his newly gained runesword and grinned. "Now, Hathor, are you happy?" The troll rolled his eyes and then shrugged.

CHAPTER
10
Westwoods

That night, the group gathered beneath the carved pillar, built an exceptionally large fire, and rats as well as men were posted strategically around the perimeter of the camp to provide ample warning should another band of goblins appear from under the Mistwall. The night was long and freezing cold, but fortunately, no raiders came. However, when the grey morning crept across the damp winter skies, they discovered that the three thieves had vanished—along with many of their pots and pans, and all of the remaining gold bars under the grain. Purkins was beside himself with rage and wanted to immediately set out after the villains, even though they had left no trail. Cal and Hathor had to hold him down.

Endril went to his baggage, opened a small leather bag which hung from his saddle, and produced a fat pouch. "Here, my friend." He shook the bag, and gold coins clanked richly within. "This is more than what the thieves took from you." He tossed the bag to a wide-eyed Purkins, who began to protest. "And I'll hear none of your objections!" said the elf with a mock frown. "Since Trondholm, the four of us have come into more than enough riches. You'll be doing my horse a favor by lightening his load!"

Purkins frowned for a moment, glancing in the direction of the Mistwall, certain that was where the thieves had fled. He sighed, tossed the bag of coins in the air, snatched it back quickly, and winked knowingly at Endril. "Thanks!" Blackie let out a gleeful cheer and dove into the pile of grain on the wagon.

A hasty breakfast was prepared, for the king was anxious to be on the move. The team was hitched and the mounts saddled. Philemus took a seat on the wagon beside Purkins, though his two servants were less than pleased to find themselves sharing the back of the wagon with Blackie and all the rats. The War Beasts were roped together and tethered to the back of the wagon. At last all was ready, and they started down the narrow, rock-strewn track that led out of the hills.

After an hour they came to the scene of the battle between the goblins and the king's men. The bodies of the vile creatures lay half frozen in grotesque positions on the ground where they had fallen. Purkins stopped his rig, and Philemus and Cal hopped down to gather up the best of the swords and a pair of halfway decent round shields. The equipment was tossed onto the wagon.

Cal then paused for a moment and surveyed the fallen goblins. "Should we not take the time to bury these dead?" he asked.

The king opposed the suggestion. "Stay here much longer and there will be many hundreds more! Then you could add our frozen corpses to this pile."

"Subhuman vermin such as that heap of dung," snapped Moorlock, "are beneath our dignity!" The prince spurred his horse into a gallop and rode on down the trail alone.

"He bears the forces of the Dark Lord no love," said the king as he followed Moorlock down the path. "He lost his family and his lands to such unspeakable creatures." The others followed silently.

In due time they reached the bent tree and turned onto the main road. A soft, quiet snow began to fall, somewhat obscuring the boiling clouds of the Mistwall, so ominously visible just a short distance to the west. Endril stopped his horse by the roadside and looked longingly into the murky cloud, seeing in his memory the now ruined beechwood he had learned to love. Just two short winters ago he had talked with and slept among those trees. Bith rode alongside, noting her friend's melancholy countenance.

"Look away, Endril. 'Twill do you no good to brood on what's lost." She touched him gently on the cheek and brushed some snowflakes out of his hair. Hathor rode by, crunching absently on a thick root. The sound brought the elf out of his dark mood. He smiled at the girl and then rode on through the falling snow.

As they neared the ogre roadblock, they began to encounter ominous, snow-covered piles beside the road. Bith eyed them suspiciously.

"It looks like bodies," she said in disgust.

Hathor stopped crunching his root and edged his horse closer to the pile. The troll leaned uneasily over in his saddle and grunted, then reached into the snowy heap and pulled out something. He held it up and dusted off the snow. It was a black leather helmet, which he tossed unceremoniously back. "More dead goblins," he said coolly. "Big battle here."

A flat bugle blatted in the distance, and the wagon and the procession stopped. Ahead of them, Govorn and a group of ogres tramped out from behind their barricade and began an animated conversation with the king, pointing first this way then another, obviously describing the recent skirmish with the goblins—goblins that now lay heaped in mounds around the battlefield. One of the ogres spotted the War Beasts tied behind the wagon and nudged Govorn. The chief ogre's jaw fell open. Instantly, he and his companions fell silent and came marching back to where the War Beasts were strung out behind Purkins' wagonload of rats and grain. Govorn's eyes were aflame with greed.

"Carthean War Beasts!" he snarled. "We gotta have them!" He grabbed one of the huge animals by the ear and stroked its shaggy fur almost lovingly. The beast snorted and rolled its eyes.

The king came trotting up to Govorn, his sword clanking at his side. "The beasts belong to our sorceress here," he said calmly. "They are not mine to give, I'm afraid."

The ogre was beside himself, having discovered a treasure worth even more to him than gold. He frowned, as deep in thought as an ogre can possibly get, and then, turning a canny eye to Geoffry, held up three huge fingers. "Give us beasts, we fight three moons!" The other ogres looked at each other and nodded eagerly in agreement. They too had begun to stroke and fondle the huge horned animals.

The king looked to Bith, and the girl stared back, showing no emotion.

She shrugged. "That's fine with me! Especially if they can be used against the Dark Lord." Govorn snarled happily and untied the beasts. He and his companions mounted their newfound treasures and raced back to the ogre camp at a thundering gallop, whooping and hollering as they went.

"Ethelrud, and I both thank you, Elizebith of Morea," Geoffry said graciously.

"I really had no idea what we were going to do with those things anyway," she said with a smile.

The ogres, overjoyed with their new acquisitions and fearful that the king might change his mind, quickly opened the barricade, and the expedition rode through to the east. The snow was beginning to fall more heavily, and Bith, wearing only a light cloak, was wet and chilled. Cal saw this and took one of the fine blankets left by the old man from the wagon and rode up to her side.

"Here, put this around you," he said with concern.

The girl looked up, somewhat in disbelief. Her red cheeks and nose, and the chattering of her teeth, revealed just how cold she really was. She brushed some melting snow from her nose and gratefully took the proffered blanket.

Bith stared after Cal as the boy turned away and rode ahead to speak with Philemus. She sighed and shrugged, wondering why she felt this way about him, and more importantly, how he felt about her. Would the memory of his lost love, Yvaine, cloud his vision forever?

They came to the junction at Roanwood, and here there was to be a sad parting. Purkins, Blackie, and the rats were returning to their stable, while the four heroes were to travel south with Geoffry, to discover just exactly what it was they were to do to save the world. They pulled off the road into a pleasant glade of evergreens, found some dry wood, and built a crackling fire. The last of the food the old man had given them was shared by all, and the four heroes made their farewells to Purkins. When it was time to leave, Bith called Blackie to her, lifted him up, and looked into his beady little rat eyes.

"I want to thank you for all that you did for us back there in that cave. You are a very brave adventurer."

The rat tugged shyly at his tail, for once at a loss for words. "Aw shucks, it weren't nuttin'." The girl kissed him on the tip of his whiskered nose. The rat puffed up his chest. "An' jus' you remember, anytime ya needs me, I'll be there fer ya!"

Elizebith put the little fellow on her lap and slipped a fine gold bracelet from her slender wrist. "This won't be a perfect fit, but you may find it useful someday." She slipped it over Blackie's head. It fit him like a necklace.

He pulled at it with his paw. "So, er, what's this? Magic or somethin'?"

"Let's just say it will bring you good luck."

"Well, hey, thanks!"

"C'mon, Blackie!" It was Purkins. The rat hopped from Bith to Endril, then to Cal, and finally to Hathor, then leaped into the wagon, which was already bouncing across the glade toward the road. They waved one last time, and many tiny rat paws in the now diminished pile of grain, now covered with a layer of snow, waved back.

• • •

"And now," droned the speaker, in a boring monotone, "I have the honor to present the four heroes, late of Trondholm, where last we stopped the Dark Lord!" Since Cairngorm had fallen under the Mistwall, the four were no longer referred to as the heroes of Cairngorm for obvious reasons. Cal, Endril, Hathor, and Bith stood up and smiled uneasily to the applause that filled the smoky hall. They sat at the head table in the great hall of Castle Glencoe, and seated at two long tables along each wall were hundreds of nobles, lesser dignitaries, and their wives.

The hall was cold, despite the many open fires that burned in the center of the room. The smoke from those fires and the many torches that lined the walls climbed to the ceiling, where some of it made its way out the vents placed there for that purpose. Most of it, however, spread through the hall, burning the eyes of all present and adding to the general torpor caused by the plentiful food and wine.

Hathor was miserable in the fancy suit the tailors had made for him, and he looked beseechingly at Bith, as if there might be something she could do to get him out of the crowded, smoke-filled room. The girl's eyes were watering, and she too was uncomfortable. Endril was not the least interested in the silly ceremonies, and was anxious to be about their task, whatever that may be. Only Cal seemed to be enjoying himself, as he sat with Philemus among a group of warrior knights, all of whom listened with avid interest to Cal's tales of the runeswords he had won and lost in his short lifetime.

At long last, King Ethelrud stood up and made a final toast to success, then bid farewell to those present. Geoffry led the way, and, without waiting, Bith and the others quickly followed the two kings out the door and into the relative fresh air of the cold stone corridor. Cal, of course, remained behind, and Endril went back and literally dragged the boy away from the table.

"Hey, I wasn't finished. . . ." Cal protested.

"We'd all have been finished if we had stayed in that hall any longer," gasped Bith as she leaned against the grey stone wall.

"No air," choked Hathor, tugging at his fancy collar till it popped open, sending a glittering pin flying across the corridor. "Aaah! Hathor breathe now."

Geoffry, noticing that the four had stopped, came back and motioned for them to follow. They were led down a dimly lit passageway to a narrow stone stair, which spiraled up around the wall of a circular tower. There was no hand-rail, so all stayed close to the wall as they climbed higher and higher. At last, Geoffry ushered them into a small room, which was hung with tapestries and warmed by a properly vented fire at one end of the room. A grey-bearded man in red silk robes sat behind a massive black oak table. He stood up as they approached.

The man's skin was pale, almost green in the firelight, and he looked to be hundreds of years old. "Greenlock! That's what they call me." The man smiled and extended a feeble old hand toward the chairs. "Please, gentles, be seated and make yourselves comfortable." Geoffry walked round and sat down next to the grey-green man.

"Greenlock is, perhaps, the oldest, the wisest, and possibly the last of the great mages left on this side of the Mistwall," Geoffry said with pride.

Bith leaned forward in awe. "Your name is a legend to me," she said in earnest.

Greenlock returned the compliment. "So, too, is yours to me, my lovely." He cocked his head to one side. "Well! It's—It's uncanny!" The old man paused and stared into Elizebith's silver eyes. "How you do resemble your mother! I knew her well before. . . ." His voice tapered off. Bith's mother now worked on the wrong side of the Mistwall, yet another servant of the Dark Lord.

Greenlock sighed. "Never lost her charms, that woman. If I didn't know better, I'd swear you were—"

"Elizebith's resemblance to her mother once fooled Schlein," said Endril.

"Got us out of quite a scrape," added Cal, remembering the time Bith had posed as her mother, first charming the wizard, then setting fire to his camp.

"Well I can imagine," replied Greenlock. "Schlein!"— he frowned—"What a stinker!" The four agreed with that sentiment and they chatted amicably with the old wizard for some time.

Finally the old mage got down to business and unrolled a brittle old scroll on the table before them.

"You have heard, no doubt, of the mythical city of Abaton?" The four looked at one another, and all save Endril shook their heads. "Unh, hmmm," Greenlock commented. "And of the fabled Stone of Time that lies within?"

Endril spoke. "The city and Stone are, from all I have heard, just what you have called them, a myth and a fable, things which do not really exist."

"Aach!" Greenlock pointed a finger in the air. "That is exactly what I thought too, and I would say that today, had I not stumbled, quite by accident, through the gates of that very city." The old mage stopped talking, poured himself a cup of wine with shaky hands, drank deeply, and plunked the cup back down on the table.

"Oh, pardon me! Would you care for a glass?" He looked from one to another. "No?" A puzzled look then crossed his face and he scratched his head. "Now, where was I . . . ? Oh yes, Abaton." Greenlock went on to describe the city, with its tall white towers topped with golden domes. He spoke longingly of the many beautiful women who lined the streets, waiting for their husbands to come home. He rambled on, describing the fat man who called himself the caliph, and how the man was always worried about one thing or another.

"And what about the Stone of Time?" asked Endril, after letting the old mage wander off the subject for several minutes. "Did you see the Stone?"

"Well . . . not exactly." Greenlock poured another glass of wine, this time more unsteadily than before. "But I know it is there; the caliph told me so himself! He keeps it in a secret tower! Way up high . . ." He waved a gnarled finger in a circle in front of his nose. "The caliph was always worried . . ."

Greenlock, now quite drunk, talked gibberish about green snakes and purple toads in a big fountain, then passed out on the table.

"You must make allowances," said Geoffry. "He was very great in his time!" The king then spoke, telling the four how it would be their job to first find the city of Abaton, the city that was always just over the horizon. How they must then gain the Stone of Time and learn how to use it. And finally, he told how they must change the past so that the Dark Lord would not come to exist.

Endril whistled, Cal shook his head in disbelief, and Hathor grabbed the wine bottle and chugged the remainder.

"You're not expecting much of us, are you?" Bith said incredulously.

"You are the only ones who can do the job," countered the king. "Old Greenlock will never find the city again." He pulled the parchment out from under the sleeping mage's nose, rolled it up, and handed it to Bith. "Take this scroll; it's what he used to get there. May it take you there too." Geoffry stood and began to pace around the table.

"You have seen how the Mistwall is on the move, not just near Cairngorm, but in many places, all along the frontier." He stopped in front of the fire, and brushed his blond hair out of his eyes. "Ethelrud and I have mustered the best of the armies and the finest magicians in the land. But I fear that this time it is not going to be enough. We may slow the progress of the Dark Lord, but we cannot stop him any longer."

Geoffry turned and faced the four, deadly serious. "*You* must go back. You must find the Dark Lord's foul beginning, and somehow put a stop to him. Before he ever existed."

The four looked at one another in disbelief. Finally Cal stood up and unsheathed the runesword. It glittered brilliantly in the firelight. "This ought to help us!" He whirled it over his head with a mighty flourish.

"Heaven help us," mumbled Bith quietly.

"Good idea," said the troll.

CHAPTER
11
To Abaton

It was a strange assembly seated round the long table. Even Schlein, who held the seat of honor, thought so. On his left sat three giants clad in musty furs; and next to them were goblin kings, each claiming to be ruler of the others. To his right were several smelly hill trolls, each the leader of a substantial clan of fighters; and on their right, there was a small deputation of strangely dressed humans whose bodies were painted blue with woad. These were the leaders that would carry the Mistwall forward for the Dark Lord. Schlein shook his head in disgust, attempting to blot out the din of invective that had followed a sharp dispute between the giants and the trolls.

His personal command of the current advance had come to an end, and it was his job to put the best of those present in charge. The Dark Lord had made it quite clear to Schlein that his only task would be to find and deliver a magic stone. An ale-filled mug flew across the room and crashed against the wall. Schlein banged his fist on the table and stood up.

"Enough of this! Hottar, sit down! Snaefthg, get out

from under the table! All of you SHUT UP! Or by the gods, I'll—" Schlein made a threatening pass with his left hand. The quarrelsome assembly fell to their seats. From Schlein's clenched fist there burst a brilliant white flash, followed by a tremendous thunderclap. The pyrotechnic display had the desired effect. There was immediate and complete silence.

"Now," said Schlein coolly, "against my better judgment, I have been forced to make certain decisions regarding the forthcoming campaign. I have made up my mind. All you have to do is listen . . . and obey." He began walking slowly around the table, twisting with one hand a piece of gold jewelry that hung on his massive bare chest. "Thidluke, you and your seers will join *and cooperate with* Snaefthg in the attacks on Roanwood. That means Snaefthg is in command of all four goblin armies!"

Three of the goblin kings made to protest, but Schlein had reached their end of the table and was glowering into their faces, just waiting for a sign of dissension, to smash the culprit into a pulp. The wizard continued, turning to point at the largest of the giants. "Hottar, you drink too much, and you talk too much, but you are the best. You will lead the giants to the Westwood. . . . Not a word from you, Borvar, if you want to live long enough to die in battle."

Schlein stopped behind the seated trolls. "You Gierroni, will lead the trolls, and cover the southern flank for Hottar. I'll let the two of you work out the details." He completed his circuit of the table and crashed down once more into his chair. "See my armorer if you need any additional equipment; there's a good deal of booty coming in right now. Any questions?" He obviously did not expect a reply, and happily, received none.

"Good! Now out of here! All of you . . . No, Thidluke, you stay; we need to talk about that spell!" There was a lot of grumbling as the chairs were pushed back, and the room slowly emptied of its gruesome occupants. Only those Schlein had put in charge seemed the least bit satisfied, and as soon as the room was clear and the door closed, a fight broke out in the hall beyond.

Schlein paid no mind to the fracas outside, for he desperately needed a way to find Elizebith and her companions, and Thidluke had suggested a way. He listened intently as the blue-painted hag outlined her idea. It involved an ancient ceremony, and a crown that she would have to buy from her sister. Schlein would sooner do away with both Thidluke and her sister, but, for the moment, they could be of use.

"You must come alone to my lodge in the Red Mountains, where I will do the deed." She rubbed her chin with her fingers. "And do not forget, you must bring the gold."

Schlein nodded absently and then smiled. He would do away with Thidluke *after* she had helped him.

It was an hour before dawn, and the snow glowed yellow in the torchlight. Most of the city was asleep, save the watchful guards and the small crowd gathered near the stable. The horses paced nervously, anxious to be moving, while their riders spoke one last time with Geoffry.

"You must travel both south and east at your best speed," said the king. "And remember to use the parchment Greenlock gave you—Do you have it?"

Bith pulled a rolled-up bundle from under her blanket and waved it at him without a word.

"Very good! I'm sure you'll be in Abaton shortly."

"Let's away!" Cal said enthusiastically.

"May the gods protect you!" said Alison, Geoffry's charming wife, who had come down to see the heroes off. Bith could think of one god in particular who had better be doing just that, and his name was spelled V-i-l-i!

The horses began to plod slowly through the snow, and the small crowd of well-wishers waved one last time. Philemus had chosen to stay and fight in the defense of Westwood at the side of Moorlock. The warrior bid farewell to the sorceress who had brought him back to life.

Out the south gate the four rode, without ceremony, and the huge iron gates slammed shut quickly enough with their passing. The road was dark, but with Endril's torch and the reflective snow on the ground, they were able to keep to the road. They rode the same horses given them by Rotherham, and Hathor no longer had need of any magic—his horse had gotten used to the smell of troll. No one spoke as they wound their way through the snow into a small pine forest, then through a clearing and past several plowed fields.

When the usual dreary grey dawn arrived, the four had put a good distance between themselves and Castle Glencoe. Hathor reached into his pack and finally broke the silence by crunching on one of the many roots he had packed for the trip.

"Our journey would be easier if we had Gunnar Grey-beard along to tell one of his travel tales," remarked Cal absently. "I was particularly fond of the one about the King of the North and his flying ship."

"Perchance you could bore us with one of those lurid tales you were spinning last night about your runeswords," Bith said sarcastically. "That would make our trip even longer and more unendurable."

Cal ignored her, and the silence, punctuated by crunching, returned.

They came to a crossroads and turned south, riding through a series of rolling hills. The snow-covered land was dotted with little farm cottages and neat stone fence rows. Had there not been the urgency of their mission and the horrid threat of war, Bith would have thought the scene most charming.

They stopped once, early in the afternoon, at a small inn, where the horses could be watered and fed, and the four enjoyed a warm fire and hot, if not tasty, bowls of gruel. Endril inquired about Abaton, but the innkeeper had never heard of the place.

When night came, they rode up to a small farmhouse, and for a small fee, were allowed to stay in the barn. Bith objected at first, until Endril pointed out just how much warmer a pile of straw was than a snow drift, which was her alternative.

The next day was brightened by a rare show of sunlight, which not only warmed their spirits, but also melted some of the snow, turning the road into a muddy mess that slowed the horses. Bith spent much of the day studying her new spellbook, this time stopping now and then to try out what she was learning. With her first effort she brought down a tall oak tree with the snap of her finger. A sight which saddened Endril, until she clapped her hands and restored the tree to its former state.

Later, Bith had Hathor roll up a snowball as tall as himself. She then read some words, and the thing burst into flames and melted away. The girl was most pleased, however, when she discovered that she could manipulate a sphere of protection. When she cast it, the sphere enveloped the four within an invisible barrier which kept out all sound and even the cold for almost an hour.

"Good spell," Hathor said appreciatively when it finally dissipated. "Use in battle. Keep us safe."

"Can we strike through it, I wonder?" asked Cal.

Bith shrugged. "It doesn't say in the book. Next time, see if you can chop through it with your new sword."

She cast the spell again. This time Endril fired an arrow at a nearby tree and it flew straight and true to the mark. They stopped near a fallen tree beside the road and Cal dismounted, assaulting the dead wood with his sword. He chopped it quickly to kindling.

"I guess that answers my question," he said with a smile. But he did not smile as he sheathed the runesword. It was a fine sword. Of that, there was no doubt. But something about this one felt a little different from the runeswords he had held before. Something was missing.

Endril suggested one further experiment, and Bith cast the spell for a third time, this time with the elf outside the protective sphere. He first threw rocks, which bounced

harmlessly away. He then reached into a special quiver by
his saddle and produced a magic arrow. Endril notched it
to his bow and took aim.

"Be ready to dodge, lest this pass through!" he warned.
Cal waved defiantly and held up his shield. He needn't
have bothered, for the arrow too, smacked into the invisible
barrier and broke into pieces.

As the sun began to fade, Bith put away her magic book
and pulled out the scroll given her by Greenlock. There was
a good chance that they might spy Abaton this evening and
she wanted to be in the proper frame of mind.

"Keep your eyes open," she warned the others. "Be on
the lookout for—What was it he said? Tall white towers,
just over the horizon."

From that moment on, they rode more slowly, squinting
in every direction, trying to make every rock and tree in the
distance into something that it wasn't. The search revealed
no Abaton, however, and when dark closed in on them,
they found themselves in the middle of a snowy cornfield
without a house or an inn in sight. Shivering, the four rode
on through the darkness for over an hour, till at last they
came to a small village. It was a welcome surprise to find
that the village elder had heard tales of the four heroes, and
went out of his way to make them comfortable.

The next day was also graced by a visit from the sun, as
though the farther they got from the Mistwall, the happier
the world became. Once again, near sunset, Bith got out the
scroll, and they all began to search. They had ridden only
a short distance when Endril let out a yell and pointed to
the east.

"There it is, just to the left of those trees—see!"

The others strained their eyes but saw nothing.

"We must ride in that direction at once!" declared the
elf. They turned from the road and set out across the field.
After a short distance, Hathor could see the spires in the
distance. They splashed through a small stream and climbed
a low hill, where they halted. At last, all four beheld the

vision. Far, far, away, just visible on the horizon, were six towers topped with onion-shaped domes. Their color was not discernible through the haze.

"How can we be sure this is Abaton, and not just some other city?" asked Cal.

"No city in this land has such towers," said Endril, his eyes still fixed on the distant vision.

"Well, we will know soon enough if we ride for the place," Bith said, with a frown on her face. "And if it keeps moving away from us, we're going to have to figure out a way to make it stop!"

They rode down the hill, through a small wood, and then across a cow pasture and stopped once more. It was getting darker, and the city in the mist was just as far away as it had been when they first saw it.

Bith clutched the scroll in her hands and chanted the words to a spell she thought might help. They rode on and on, through more fields and forests, chasing the elusive vision, but to no avail. Night had fallen and there was just a sliver of the moon to light their way. The discouraged four continued on till they came to a lonely farm, where they spent the night in yet another barn.

The next morning the clouds were back, and wintry winds swept across the empty fields. With vague instructions from their suspicious host, the four struggled back to what resembled a road, and traveled on to a village. The innkeeper there had actually heard of Abaton, but never seen it. After lunch, Endril pushed the plates aside and rolled open a map of the realm, to study the situation.

The elf pointed as the others watched intently. "Here we are—Raskilde, see? And over here, not many leagues distant, lies the ocean."

"Fine," said Cal. "We're close to the sea. So what?"

"So this. Later when we catch our glimpse of Abaton, we will ride so that it is between us and the sea. Then we will close in on the city." He traced an arc on the map.

"Won't the city just disappear into the ocean?"

Endril shrugged. "Well, we'll find that out soon enough. Do you have a better plan?"

"Not at the moment." Cal put his mug to his lips and finished his ale.

Later, as the grey day began to darken, the four again sighted their elusive quarry, almost directly between them and the sea. Endril was pleased, for they had no need to sidetrack. Immediately they set out in the direction of the city at a gallop, this time following, more or less, a road that twisted back and forth but led generally in the right direction.

Night found them walking their horses slowly down the beach, toward the lights of a fishing village. Abaton had vanished somewhere between them and the ocean.

Cal turned to Endril, who was riding alongside, "We need a new plan."

"I know," said the elf calmly.

That night, around the fireside of yet another inn, it was Hathor who finally came up with the definitive plan. He stood up suddenly after a long silence, and leaned heavily over the map.

"Have idea," he stated simply. "There four of us. Four points on compass." His fat finger pointed to the compass shown on Endril's map. "We go apart." He traced four paths. "We come back together. City in middle."

It was so simple, Bith slapped her head for not having thought of it herself. They studied the map further and laid their new plan.

In the morning Bith tore the parchment into four separate pieces, and gave one to each of the others. They stood together in a small circle for a moment, holding one another's hands while Bith chanted a small spell. Then they mounted up and rode off, each in a different direction, so that by sunset they would be all be at opposite points of the compass, and, hopefully, would surround Abaton.

CHAPTER
12
Searchers

Hathor shifted uneasily in his saddle, unsure that he had made the correct turn at the last intersection. His strong shaggy brown horse had come to a stop, sensing the rider's uncertainty. The troll reached under his thick cloak, pulled out his bit of the scroll, and squinted at the cryptic ink marks put on the back of the parchment by Endril. He pursed his lips, whistled, and then tugged at some of the red hair which hung down over his forehead. The last thing he wanted was for the group to fail because he couldn't read a map. Finally, Hathor decided to go with his instincts, and nudged his heels into the horse's sides. The animal plodded slowly forward along the slushy trail.

By evening, the troll had ridden many miles. His backside was sore; he hadn't eaten all day and his stomach was complaining audibly. But those discomforts paled in comparison to his great fear, the certainty that he was totally lost and that he would never see Abaton again, not even in the faraway distance. Hathor let out a low groan. He stared ahead with glazed eyes. At length, however, troll and mount came to the top of a gentle rise and he glanced across the valley below. Snow as far as he could see. A few leafless trees, curving hedgerows, a herd of dirty sheep, some small cottages . . . and . . . tall towers in the mist!

Hathor's heart skipped a beat, and in an instant, he was riding down the hill at the gallop for the distant city. As the horse splashed through a small stream, the rider lost sight of Abaton, but continued in the same direction, knowing, or at least hoping, that the vision would be there as he climbed the next low hill. Much to his relief and great amazement when they breasted the next summit, the city was not only still there, it was closer and more distinct than ever before. He could now make out the tops of the city wall, and see flags waving in the wind!

Faster than before he rode on, and the horse, who seemed quite aware of his rider's anxiety, showed no sign of tiring or slacking his rapid pace. Zig-zagging across another small valley, on and on he went. Horse and rider thundered through a small pine forest, there upsetting a small cart loaded with logs, oblivious to the curses of the unfortunate woodsman, who shook an angry fist after them. The path widened to a cart track, and the small forest was left behind.

Soon, Hathor became aware of a definite change in the world around him. As the city loomed close ahead, he noticed that the snow alongside the road was gone, and so was the cold. The troll looked around in amazement, slowing his mount to a steady trot. Overhead the ever-present grey clouds were no more, and a cheerful orange sunset was all aglow. He could see a star directly above. On either side of the path, tall green grasses rustled in a gentle, warm breeze that brought exotic aromas to Hathor's sensitive nose.

The troll pulled the thick bearskin cloak from his shoulders and draped it over the saddle, slowing his horse to a walk, and then to a stop, not ten feet from the tall, ironbound wood gate set into the side of a polished white tower. He dismounted slowly, painfully reminded that he had been in the saddle almost all day. He stretched slowly. A torch appeared high up on the wall above, and he could hear muffled voices speaking excitedly somewhere nearby. Hathor led his horse over to the gate.

"Hello inside!" He banged on the door three times with his big fist. Immediately, the great gates began to swing open to the inside. In the dim twilight, he beheld a small gathering of people, each carrying a brightly burning torch. They stood in a circle within the gate. There were men and women, all clad in flowing robes. The men were short, their hair and eyes dark. The women, and they were far more numerous than the men, were taller, and their hair flowed down over their shoulders in long, complex braids. A small yellow dog darted out from the crowd, ran quietly up to Hathor, and began sniffing at his feet. One of the men, wearing a broad gold belt around his crimson robes, stepped forward.

"Welcome to Abaton, stranger."

A small cheer went up from the others and they began to close in around the troll and his sturdy horse. The man extended a hand to Hathor. "I am called Komir, keeper of the North Gate!" He shook the troll's hand and pulled him gently within the walls, leading the crowd slowly along the street.

"Me . . . I am Hathor," the troll stammered, utterly bewildered at the friendly reception.

"I know you must be tired and hungry, my friend. We must attend to your needs—but later. Right now, the caliph is expecting you and it would never do to keep him waiting. Please follow me and I shall take you to the palace!" Komir bowed with an extravagant flourish of hands, turned, and then walked briskly through the crowd, pushing people aside. Hathor had to hurry to keep up. As they walked, other citizens of the city reached out and gently touched the troll, as if to reassure themselves that the visitor was really there and not just an illusion.

"Don't mind them," said Komir, looking back at the troll. "You are quite an attraction, you know. Visitors here are as rare as winged pigs."

The street that they traveled was paved with neatly fitted smooth stones, and lined on either side with closely packed houses that looked to Hathor as though they were made of solidified sand or dried mud—he could not be sure which. Under open, arched windows were long flower boxes, and from each box hung lush green plants and many white flowers—no doubt the source of the unfamiliar sweet scent that had wafted to his nose when he first arrived.

From within some of the houses came the strains of music. It reminded the troll of a harp he had once heard, and the sound was not unlike what had come from the ivory box Bith played at Lord Rotherham's. Komir led him through a beautiful park, filled with tall trees, the like of which Hathor had never seen. Long spike-shaped leaves shot out in great bunches at the tops of tall ringed trunks. Behind the trees was a round stone pond. Jets of water shot into the air from some unknown source and splashed merrily down a terraced sculpture in the middle. Several small children, who had been splashing noisily about, fell silent and stared at the passing visitor and the parade of citizens who followed.

"That is our fountain of youth," Komir said, noting Hathor's obvious interest.

It was night by the time they reached the white marble walls and towers of the great palace which stood at the center of the city, yet the place was well lit by torches and cressets that lined the walls and streets. Ahead was another crowd that had gathered at the base of a broad stair that led up into the palace. There were horses and riders among them. Hathor broke into a broad smile. Bith had spotted him and was waving happily. And next to her were Endril and Caltus.

• • •

"You are certain you would go through with this?" hissed the old crone, looking sideways at the great bulk of a man who sat next to her on the crude wooden throne.

Schlein held back his rage at such disrespectful insolence, and merely nodded angrily.

The old woman knelt awkwardly and lifted the lid of a small, battered wooden box. Her gnarled fingers pulled aside a red silk cloth to reveal a gleaming gold crown, brilliant even in the dim firelight of the dingy room. The floor was dirt, and the walls smoke-blackened by years of open fires. There was little in the room, no decoration, only the thick throne upon which the wizard now sat, some rude shelves along the wall, littered with bottles and jars, and the stone fire pit.

In the pit there burned a roaring fire. Atop the fire hung a huge black cauldron, wherein there boiled some disgusting mixture. She had labored over it all day, and with each added ingredient, the aroma that filled the room had grown increasingly vile. Occasionally some of the concoction would bubble over the side and ooze down into the fire, giving off a putrid stench.

Schlein absently picked at a splinter which had caught the attention of his left hand, while Thidluke, his seeress, lifted the crown. She stood again, and held it before the magician, her eyes filled with a strange gleam.

"Behold the Crown of Hylesa! The all-seeing eyes! None but the most powerful dare to wear this. . . ." She hesitated. "You are absolutely sure?"

Schlein banged his fist on the arm of the throne. "Of course I am sure, old woman. You're not dealing with any mere man! I am soon to be a god! Second only in greatness to the Dark Lord himself. Get on with it."

Thidluke extended two scrawny wode-painted arms and solemnly placed the shining crown atop the wizard's head. It was covered with ornate carvings of birds, bats, and flying dragons, and two great bat-like wings of solid gold stretched out from either side. Schlein reached up and adjusted it slightly. A grin of satisfaction twisted his face. The crown felt strangely pleasant. It obviously belonged on his head.

The old crone continued. "With this, you shall see through their eyes. You must marshal all your powers, for there will be much to see . . ."

"Yes! Yes!" Schlein interrupted impatiently, waving a hand at the woman, "You've told me all this already. I am fully prepared, both spiritually and physically. In fact"— he slapped his hand against his bare chest—"I've never been in better shape."

The old woman shook her head and shambled slowly over to the boiling cauldron. She pulled a long iron spoon from a rack and inserted it into the lumpy brew, alternately stirring and then spooning up some of the mixture for close examination. After several minutes, she stuck her finger into the mess, tasted it, and then turned and whispered, "It is ready at last."

Thidluke hung the spoon back on its rack and dropped slowly to her knees before the fire. She then began to rock from side to side, chanting in an indistinguishable monotone. White steam began to rise from within the cauldron. It thickened and turned yellow, then orange, and began to fill the room. The steam became smoke and the smoke turned black. It burned Schlein's eyes, but he kept them open, squinting and straining to watch the old woman. At last she let out an ear-piercing scream, threw up her arms, and then fell over in a slump.

From within the great cauldron came a high-pitched chattering as of a thousand tiny creatures. Then, out of it, amid the smoke, poured a torrent of tiny bats. The room was instantly filled with them, fluttering wildly about. These were no ordinary bats, either, for instead of normal heads each one had the face of a miserable human, with large red melancholy eyes. The air was so thick with bats that Schlein put his arm over his eyes to keep the horrid creatures out of his face.

The swarm of bats swirled and climbed. They found the hole in the roof and began streaming out into the swirling clouds that were the Mistwall, and more and more poured forth from the iron pot to fill the room. The swarm continued to grow, and streamed through the murk of the Mistwall in their flight to the east. The cloud of bats broke into two columns, then split again into four, and then again into eight.

Schlein suddenly winced with pain and clutched his hands desperately to his temples. The first of the bats had emerged from the mists and into the light of the world, and now in his mind, he could see everything that they saw. Dogging from tree to tree, swooping low over houses and fields, so many sights, so many visions, so much information, all coming to him at once. How could he ever assimilate all this . . . ? and the pain! Schlein closed his eyes tight, gritted his teeth, and dug his fingernails into the arms of the throne.

Philemus rode alongside Moorlock, who was brooding and silent. The recently rejuvenated warrior could easily understand the young prince's mood. For he, like Moorlock, had lost a wife, family, and country to the Dark Lord. And for Philemus it had happened so suddenly. One moment he was in quest of the Treasure of Arthana, and the next, he was in the presence of Elizebith and her three companions. He had left behind everyone and everything he had known when he had entered the cave of the Automaton. Now a hundred years later, he had little to live for . . . a man without a country, since the Mistwall had devoured his homeland.

Behind them marched a column of brave if poorly trained soldiers, the latest addition to the defenses of Westwood. For two days they had been recruiting from among the older able-bodied men of the cities, and the refugees from the lands to the west. The men were armed, albeit poorly, and all but one had warm boots and a shield. Philemus sighed. He could at least lead these men into battle, and die a true warrior's death. It was about the only solace left to him.

The troop marched out of a wood and into a busy clearing behind a makeshift wall made of logs and baskets of rocks and snow, which was being thrown up by a throng of workers even as they approached. Moorlock halted and held out his hand, pointing into the grey skies beyond the wall.

"What do you make of that?"

Philemus, jarred from his thoughts, squinted but could see nothing. "What is it?" he asked, tugging at his short black beard.

"There, beyond those trees."

The tiny dots swirled like bits of dust blown about in the wind and came closer. It was a steady stream of birds, or bats . . . That was it! Bats! The cloud of bats streamed overhead. The soldiers stopped and stared, and the workers at the wall dropped what they were doing and watched in disbelief, all present wondering what new plague was coming at them from behind the Mistwall.

CHAPTER
13
The Stone

"Allow me to offer you the hospitality of our fair city,"
said the red-faced man seated on the pile of cushions. He
wore a blue silk gown, embroidered with golden flowers,
and pointed yellow slippers stuck out beneath his crossed
legs. A small stubble of a beard covered his face, but the
sincere smile on his face left no doubt that he was truly
glad to see the four heroes. This was Nabona, the Caliph
of Abaton, and, in spite of their desire to find the Stone
of Time, they had no choice but to attend this welcoming
ceremony.

The others, like Hathor, had ridden all day without food,
and then closed in on the city with disbelief. Upon arrival,
each been escorted in a similar manner to the central palace
by a keeper of the gate. Now they were all seated on plush
cushions on the floor before the caliph, smack in the center
of an enormous room. It was filled with marble pillars and
arched ceilings. Every few feet there were large potted
trees, so many in fact, that it made Endril feel as though
he were sitting in the midst of a small forest. Seated beneath
every tree was a group of robed women with long, braided

hair. They smiled, talked among themselves, and watched the proceedings with great interest.

Nabona rubbed his hand over his balding head and then waved a hand in the direction of a low table, piled high with food of all sorts—fruit, vegetables, large and small loaves of bread, and cheeses of every kind.

"As the Caliph of Abaton, it is my duty and honor to welcome noble guests such as yourselves. Now, I am aware that introductions can sometimes be long and tedious, so we can take care of those formalities over the banquet table. You must all be hungry, in need of baths, and weary. In that order, we shall attend to your needs." He struggled to his feet from within his mound of pillows and led the way to the feast. "Please, come savor the fruits of our modest farms!"

Hathor needed no invitation, surveyed the spread, and set instantly upon a mound of enormous turnips, the largest he had ever seen, each one over two feet long and as thick as a log. Amid the troll's loud crunching, the others followed suit. Endril selected some crisp green apples that resembled melons in size, Bith took up slices of rich yellow cheese and a small salted loaf of bread, while Cal dug into a basketful of deep red berries of a type he had never seen before. They were soon joined by all the other spectators in the room—the lovely women, who turned out to be the nobility, or what was left of it, of Abaton.

As they ate, introductions were made, and each of the four was, in turn, introduced personally to Nabona and then to the heads of the houses of Abaton. The introductions took over an hour, and Hathor, whose interest in meeting everyone was, at best, marginal, was exceedingly glad that all was taking place round the table.

"You will note," said the caliph, having cornered Endril, "that we have no meat in our diet. Long ago, we discovered that we could not afford such a luxury, for a cow is much more valuable for the milk and cheese it gives. You see, our city is surrounded by such a small belt of arable land, every inch of it must be carefully farmed to serve our needs."

"Most interesting," said the elf—and then he leaned forward—"and your cheeses are very rich and satisfying. But what intrigues me most is the very nature of your fair city? How is that this place is so hard to reach?"

"A good question, indeed," answered Nabona. "That is a tale that could take many years in the telling," of which remark the elfs eyebrows rose.

The caliph continued quickly. "Yet I shall endeavour to relate it to you as briefly and succinctly as possible . . . starting now!" He waved his hand, and two servants rushed out of the background, tossing cushions strategically on the marble floor as Nabona sat down without even looking, knowing full well that pillows would be there beneath him before his ample posterior arrived.

"It all began many many centuries ago, possibly long before you were even born." The caliph raised an eyebrow, "I've read that you elves live remarkably long lives."

Endril smiled. "Quite possibly."

"Well, anyway, the city around us was not always detached from time and floating about the world. Long, long ago, one of my beloved ancestors, one Ibn an Nabona reigned as absolute lord of the greatest desert kingdom ever known. It was blessed with many fair cities, all filled with elegant palaces. There were three great rivers, whose waters gave life to the many farms in the desert around them. To the east and west were trade routes to fabled lands, all bustling with fat caravans that brought spices, cloth, gems, and riches to the land."

Nabona paused as a servant brought them each a tall glass of herbal wine. Endril wanted to refuse, but as he sniffed the bouquet, the aroma of spring flowers could not be resisted, and he drank deeply with the caliph. In a moment a warm glow permeated his body, and the two were feeling much happier. Nabona continued.

"As was the custom then, during the New Year's festival, Ibn, to prove his divine right to rule, was required to give up his office, only to receive it again from the priests of the god Marduk, after rites of humiliation." A sad look came into Nabona's eyes, and he shook his head.

"For some reason—I personally think there was treachery involved—the priests failed to return with the pollen from the tree of life. Ibn an Nabona was not restored to office and mysteriously disappeared in a desert sandstorm. The history speaks of a day when the sun went out, and soon thereafter the land was set upon by winged wolves that flew down upon the kingdom with a cold north wind. There followed drought, and with it, famine and death. The sheep and goat herds, which supported the populace, perished miserably."

The caliph gestured to a servant, who brought more wine. "And then the worst happened. The goat god, Aliddo, was filled with rage, and in a fit of anger took his revenge directly upon the city of Abaton, setting it adrift in both time and space." Nabona looked sadly at the floor. "Ever since that moment, we, the citizens, have existed in no place— never here, never there—always between the sunset and the dawn, drifting without rhyme or reason from one continent to another, eternal wanderers searching for a place to be."

Cal, who had been listening intently nearby, let out a low whistle. "Have you no trade or commerce with the rest of the world?" asked the boy.

Nabona shook his head sadly. "Nary a stick nor a bundle. We are totally self-sufficient, and thank the gods for that. But we continually endeavor to get in touch with the outside world. Twice a year, the bravest of the men of Abaton volunteer to go out into the world in order to establish contact with someone—anyone—But do they return?" He sighed and rolled his brown eyes. "Never. They never return."

Cal leaned closer, wide-eyed. "They never return?"

" 'Tis true. You see it is quite easy to leave. You go out the gate, and disappear into the haze. Always our men go forth into the world, there to reestablish our connection, but thus far none have succeeded. We remain in isolation."

"That would explain why all your nobles are female," Cal said, more to himself than anyone in particular.

The caliph smiled and winked, then went back to his pretense of sadness. "Alas, I fear that is so, young man. And visitors from the outside are . . . so rare, so few and far between, as to be considered miracles. You four have just quadrupled the number of outsiders who have come to us during my lifetime."

Endril was intrigued by this. "Only one other visitor in your lifetime besides us?" asked the elf.

The caliph nodded slowly. "Only one . . . a rather strange fellow with a white beard. Called himself Greenrock, or frock, or something like that."

Cal glanced at Endril.

"But the poor fellow was only here one night . . . came by some kind of magic. Oh, if I only knew how! Got drunk on our wine and then disappeared the next morning." Nabona frowned at the two. "You're not planning to do the same thing, are you?"

Cal patted the man on the shoulder. "No, no, we came here for a reason!"

"We plan to stay for a while," said Endril reassuringly.

"Well, you have given us hope. For if you have managed to reach us, others may too. You must tell me, tomorrow, exactly how you managed to find us."

Just then three buxom women sat down beside Cal and began stroking his muscular arms. In a moment Bith appeared, circling around the young warrior like a vulture, and drove the women away with an evil glare.

Elizebith had been looking all night for an opportunity to swing the conversation around to the object of their quest, but as the evening wore on, she found herself quite unable to broach the subject, as no one, not the caliph nor any of the noblewomen to whom she was introduced, would even listen when she mentioned the Stone of Time.

And then there was another irritation—these women. Bith fumed. For one thing there were too many of them,

and for another, they were just too interested in Cal, and
for that matter, Endril and Hathor as well. Time and again,
Elizebith worked her way between one of her companions
and one or another silken-robed beauty, just in time to stop
an indiscretion before it could happen.

The party dragged on for what seemed like an eternity to
Bith, and didn't break up until long past midnight. At last,
the four were taken by servants to their separate rooms,
where they were bathed and then tucked in for the night
under silk sheets.

When her attendants had left, and the candle was snuffed
out, Bith sighed with relief and relaxed under the luxurious
sheets, stretching her aching body. The tropical night was
most welcome. Tomorrow would be soon enough to find the
Stone, she thought to herself, and promptly fell asleep.

Into an attic, down in a cave, fleeing an eagle, stopping to rest in a barn, following the innumerable flights
of others across a frozen lake, crashing into a tree, falling
weak to the snow, pursued by weasels—these were but a
few of the multiplicity of sights, sounds, smells, fears,
and feelings that flashed through Schlein as he wore the
crown. Again he pressed his hands heavily against his
temples in a futile effort to relieve the pain. In the brief
moments when he could think, he chastised himself for
his arrogance. Nearly a god he might be, but not even a
god could handle all the sensory input that flooded into
his head.

The wizard squirmed back and forth on the rude wooden
throne—the rough finish quite appropriate for its miserable
occupant. Minutes of agony drifted slowly past, and the
smoke from the cauldron ceased. At the same time, the last
of the bats issued forth and flew up out the roof. Thidluke
still lay limp on the floor, but Schlein was too blinded by
visions and too busy to notice or care.

After what seemed like hours, but was, in reality, just
minutes, the wizard finally began to discern vague patterns

in the torrent of visual input from the numberless throng of
bats through whose eyes he was seeing. Little by little, he
began to blot out the unimportant, the insignificant, and the
mundane, so that he was able to concentrate on the broad
picture which was unfolding across the lands beyond the
Mistwall.

Inside his tormented brain, he became dimly aware of
the feverish preparations around Westwoods, even saw the
ogre barricade by Roanwood . . . but such things were not
foremost on his mind. His one and only goal was to find
Elizebith of Morea, the four who had so often thwarted him,
and the Stone of Time, whatever that might be.

Something deep inside him stirred. What was it? A flash,
a glimpse. It happened again, a swarm of images that
he struggled to bring together into some kind of whole.
Part of him knew this was what he was looking for, and
Schlein tightened his lips and strained to blot out ever
more of the useless and see only that which he sought.
Through a thousand eyes he now saw Elizebith, riding a
horse . . . and the elf, the troll, and the boy. . . . Riding to
a common goal. What was that place? Clouded by haze, it
was totally unfamiliar to him, white walls and towers. Four
gates opened. . . .

The effort was too great, even for a would-be god, and
the pain overwhelmed Schlein. All went black, and he fell
forward out of the wooden throne and crashed unconscious
to the dirt floor. Fortunately for him, the crown which was
both the source of his distant sight and of his torment, came
loose and bounced free.

Thidluke, whose dim eyes had been secretly watching,
cursed under her breath. He had escaped the crown, and
would probably live.

"I tell you there is no such thing. The mere idea is
preposterous. If we had such a thing here, do you not
think we would use it to rescue ourselves from this life
of eternal exile!"

"And I happen to know it *is* here somewhere!" insisted Bith. She and the others were seated at a table located in an arched-roof court adjacent to a reflecting-pool bordered with palm trees. Bith put her hands on the table and looked Nabona in the eyes. "We came here for it. We must have it. Our world depends upon what the four of us can do with it. Please tell us, where is the Stone?"

Throughout breakfast the caliph ducked and evaded Bith, who had done most of the talking. And despite every argument she put forth, he stubbornly maintained that the Stone of Time did not exist. Finally Bith got up and walked around the table, where she stood shaking her finger in Nabona's face.

"You said you wanted to know how we got here, right?"

The caliph nodded with bulging eyes, backing away from her as best he could.

"Well, listen to this. Not a one of us will tell you a thing about how we found Abaton until you give us access to the Stone of Time!"

Nabona sat speechless and perplexed. He tugged uncomfortably at his collar with his pudgy finger, and then, at last, let out a long sigh. "As you wish. As you wish. But mind you, no good can come of this. There is a reason why we locked it away these many years ago. What use you can make of it is quite beyond my understanding, and I grant you permission fully against my better judgment."

Bith gave him a little kiss on the forehead, and the caliph's face turned beet red. When breakfast was over, he personally led the group of four through the palace grounds to a square, walled building set off to one side near the outer rampart. Unlike the rest of the buildings they had seen, this one showed signs of neglect. Vines had taken root in cracks in the walls, and the arched door was secured by a rusty iron lock that obviously had not been opened for ages.

Slowly, Nabona fumbled under his robe and withdrew a large brass key. He reluctantly placed it in the key-hole.

"I haven't done this in years—I really doubt it will even . . ." Just then, there was a loud clank. The lock snapped open and fell heavily to the ground, barely missing the caliph's toes.

"Phew!" He wiped the perspiration from his brow, pushed the door open, and they walked inside. The air was stale and musty. Off to the right was a long, arched-roof hall, down which the caliph led them. The only light came from a row of small windows high up in one wall. There was no furniture, but as they proceeded, Cal noticed with interest the weapons and shields that hung along the walls. Bith took special note of the hundreds of painted frames that extended in rows from the arched ceiling to the floor. Each panel was a complete scene of life in the city she had seen outside, yet the paintings seemed to have a life of their own, and something about them disturbed her.

"Pictures make me feel funny," said Hathor.

"Turn your eyes away from them," cautioned Nabona. "Whatever you do, don't stare into them for any length of time. We'll be out of here soon enough."

Bith was about to ask about the pictures, when they stopped at a small bolted door at the far end of the hall. The caliph produced another key, and ushered them into a dark, dusty room. He pulled a lamp from atop a cabinet and rummaged around in the shelves. "Ahh, here it is." He produced a clay jar, pried off the lid, and poured oil into the lamp.

"Does anyone have flint and steel?"

Cal provided the light, and the room brightened in the yellow flame. Across the room was a stone stair.

"It's at the top of this tower. Follow me and watch your step." Up they climbed, a tiresome number of steps. Cal counted thirty flights, he thought. He was so breathless by the time they reached the top, he had lost count.

At the top was one of the onion-shaped gold domes they had seen from the distance. Inside was a plain room, bare of paintings or any other decoration. Sunlight flooded in through an arched door that led out to a small balcony. Near the center of the room sat a dust-covered couch, and next to it a small chest. Bith walked over and knelt by the chest and then looked to Nabona. He nodded.

CHAPTER
14

Odd Adventures

Bith walked slowly to the couch and wrinkled her nose. "Look at this dirt and filth!" She began pounding on the cushions to dislodge some of the years of accumulated dust and spider webs. She succeeded in filling the room with an unbreathable cloud.

"Bith! Stop!" screamed Cal.

"I already have! Sheesh!" They retreated to the balcony so the mess could settle.

"As I said," remarked Nabona, "it's been a long time since anyone has been up here."

"I'll say." Bith was shaking her hands briskly in an effort to remove the grit and cobwebs.

The others had turned their attention to the magnificent view of the city to be had from this high vantage point. Endril leaned over the stone rail and strained to see beyond the city walls, back to the lands from which they had come. There was a small area of grassland, then a blue haze, and nothing visible beyond. The caliph stood beside him and followed his gaze.

"You'll find nothing beyond the city, save our narrow

strip of pastureland. You see there the walls of the prison of Abaton." He waved his hand in a broad sweep. "It is the same in every direction."

"It's not exactly a prison," observed Cal. "I mean, you could leave if you wanted to?"

"Well, uh, yes. But if one leaves Abaton, one never returns. It is a one-way trip through that haze." Nabona leaned against the rail and laced his fingers together. "Would you leave your home if you knew you would never be able to return?"

The four looked at one another with knowing glances and as one responded, "Yes!"

"We have all done that very thing," said Bith. "The four of us are outcasts. None of us can go home."

"Can never go back again!" added the troll.

"No, no," countered Nabona. "That's not what I mean. It's not the same at all." He glanced at the door. "Anyway, the dust seems to have settled. I suppose you'll be wanting to risk your lives with that stone."

Back inside they went, and Bith sat down on the couch, ignoring the dust, and bent over the small chest. The others stood in a circle around her. It was not locked, and the leather hinges were old and rotten, so when she lifted the lid, it came loose in her hands. She put it gently aside. Inside the chest was a moth-eaten cloth bag, and part of an old scroll that had, for the most part, disintegrated with age.

Bith lifted out the paper first.

"This resembles the scroll given us by Greenlock," she said, examining both sides carefully. "The writing has faded, and it is incomplete." She compared it with the portion of scroll she had carried into the city. "Aha, they were once one." She looked at the others, "But since we could not make head or tails of the part we had, I fear this will be of no help." She held up the scroll to the caliph. He took it in his hand and looked it over top and bottom and then shrugged.

"I promised you that we would tell how we came to

Abaton if you let us use the Stone. You have part of the
means in your hand. We found the city by quartering what
we had of that scroll. Each of us carried a piece and then
separated, coming together from four different directions
until we reached your gates."

"Very interesting." Nabona frowned, looking at the piece
of scroll. "That Greenflock must have stolen this!"

"Possibly so," she continued, "but it does suggest a means
of returning to the city from outside."

Nabona's eyes lit up and he nodded gravely. He carefully
rolled up the bit of scroll and tucked it into his robe.

"But I would caution you to send out groups of four at
a time," Bith said.

"And preferably in the company of a competent magic
user," added the elf, patting the girl on the shoulder. "I think
her communion spell had a lot to do with our success."

Elizebith next lifted out the cloth bag. It was brown,
covered with dust, and tied together at the top with a
piece of gold string. When she tried to untie it, the whole
bag ripped and came apart in her hands, revealing a very
ordinary-looking rounded rock, not unlike one you might
find lying on the seashore.

She held it up for all to see. "Not a very impressive
rock, is it?"

"Maybe that's just a fake," suggested Cal. "Maybe the
real one is hidden around here somewhere."

"Check for illusion," suggested Hathor, remembering how
things had been hidden in Arthana's cave.

"Sounds worth a try . . ." Elizebith stood up with a jerk,
her silver eyes open wide, staring intently at the rock.
"Woof! I-I think not." She was suddenly breathless.

"What is it? What's wrong," asked Cal. Bith said nothing
for a moment, then took a deep breath and slowly settled
back down on the couch, holding the stone close to her
bosom.

"I feel it," Bith whispered. "I-I think I know what to do."
She lay back on the couch and pulled up her feet. Without

warning, the girl seemed to freeze in place, still clutching the stone, as though deep in a trance.

Hathor and Cal knelt by her side. The troll felt her cheek, and Cal tried to pull the stone from her hands. It wouldn't budge.

"Well, this is a puzzle. Do you think she's all right?" asked the boy.

"Still breathing," remarked Hathor, holding his fingers beneath her nose.

"What should we do?" asked Cal.

"We wait," said Endril.

Her first thought, when the stone popped out of its bag and she nearly dropped it on the floor, was that it was just a fake. This plain-looking object couldn't be the Stone of Time. Cal had to be right.

The words to a dispell illusion were on the tip of her tongue, when her hands began to tingle and the electric feeling shot through her body. Oh yes, this was magic! Magic of a power she had never before experienced. She jumped to her feet barely able to see the others.

Get hold of yourself, Bith. You are a magic-user. You have practiced for years and possess great powers of your own. . . . All you have to do is concentrate. Through supreme effort, she managed to calm herself down enough to think clearly.

Bith eased herself back down onto the couch and lay back. That felt better. Even though she had no idea what was about to happen, the thing did not feel evil. Perhaps she should just go with it and see where it would take her.

She fixed her eyes on a tiny crack overhead. Now she was becoming drowsy, and began to sink into a pleasant, warm fog. The sights of the room around her faded into a hazy twilight. Only the crack in the ceiling seemed to remain clear.

She was aware of an odd sensation, as though she were in two places at one time . . . and there was something . . .

another presence, strange sounds, smells, and voices. Suddenly she felt cold and all went black.

Bith opened her eyes slowly. Her body ached all over as though she had not slept the night before. There were cushions beneath her and she could still see the tiny crack.

Was this it? She felt sick inside. All the stone had done was rob her of her strength. She closed her eyes for a moment, they were so tired, and then struggled to sit up. Maybe Endril should see if . . . Endril! There was no Endril to be seen, nor was she in the tower any longer. Around her was the ramshackle furniture of a peasant house, and she was sitting on a straw mattress. Where was she?

She stood up. Ow! Her bare feet hurt. Bare feet? Where were her black leather shoes? Those were not Bith's feet, and this was not her dress—it was a dirty old rag! For a moment she continued to stare at herself, then a flood of foreign, yet familiar thoughts came to her. She knew there was a mirror hanging on the wall, went to it, and stared at the face that was looking back at her. The woman whose body she occupied sighed, rubbed the sleep out of one eye, and reached for a comb. Maybe she could rest more after the animals were fed.

She wondered how she knew who she was and what she was doing. It was as though she were having a dream, and knew it, yet could not wake up. She and this girl were one. Now Bith knew where she was—this was Abaton, of course, and she was now a charwoman. She was Mildred, who had worked all night scrubbing the caliph's floors. That's why her body ached. Just wait till she got her hands on Nabona—No, wait. Nabona wasn't the caliph Mildred knew, the caliph was tall and blond, and had a small rascal of a dark-haired son named Nabona. . . .

Bith wondered, Could she have traveled back in time? Was this really an earlier Abaton? She slipped into her sandals and stepped outside the door. There was a bag of grain. Instinctively she put it around her neck and began feeding the chickens that were dashing around the yard, squawking and squabbling with one another.

Now Bith wished she had done a little more research before she tried the Stone. What year had it been in Abaton when she started? Since she seemed to know and remember everything that Mildred knew, she was quite aware of when it was now. It was the Year of the Eagle, three thousand and twelve. But when was that?

She spent the rest of the morning at various farm chores, one of which involved going out the gate to tend a small herd of cows. When she saw the haze beyond the city, she experienced the fear and the lure that it instilled in Mildred's heart, and Bith knew too the sadness that infected all who lived in the exiled city.

For a moment Bith considered walking out into the haze and leaving Abaton, as she seemed to have a certain measure of control over Mildred's body. Mildred too had considered walking through the haze to the world beyond, many times. Just through the haze was escape from all the drudgery and chores. However, Bith was none too sure she would ever get back to her own time if she wandered out and lost Abaton in some other century—and quite possibly some other land as well.

Here came two of Mildred's dear friends, and they exchanged pleasantries, then set about the task of milking the cows. It was hard work. Something unfamiliar to Bith, who had spent a pampered childhood in her mother's palace, yet to Mildred it seemed almost a simple pleasure, and when she sneaked a cup to drink, the warm milk tasted quite delightful.

Evening found her celebrating the fact that she had no further work to do and would be able to sleep all night undisturbed. As Mildred lay on her pillow, staring at the tiny crack in her ceiling and wondering what tomorrow held in store, Bith wondered how she would ever return to her companions. . . . No, make that, *if* she would ever return.

Bith had been in the trance for over an hour, and Cal was getting worried. Nabona insisted he had no knowledge of what was going on and didn't know what to do.

"I warned you not to try this thing!" He shrugged. "I have matters of state to attend to. You know where to find me." He turned and walked over to the stair, then stopped at the door. "Oh, and when you come down, be careful of those paintings in the hall. I caution you once more not to stare into them." He winked. "They're magic, you know. Inform me when the girl awakens."

The caliph checked to make sure he still had the fragment of parchment inside his robe, and then hurried down the stairs, muttering to himself. The three heroes still on their feet discussed possible courses of action. Most of the ideas that Cal proposed Endril rejected, and the elf wanted to do nothing. Finally Hathor volunteered to bring a bucket of water. They would try a wet cloth on her forehead.

The wet cloth didn't work. Neither did shaking Elizebith, who was rigidly locked in her position, and when they tried to lift her from the couch, the combined strength of the three could not budge the young slip of a girl.

"She's in the grip of a powerful spell," said Endril, shaking his head. "It's best we do nothing more to disturb her." The three sat down on the floor and waited. Hathor began to doze off. Cal too found himself getting sleepy. He shook himself awake, got to his feet, and wandered out onto the balcony for some fresh air.

The warm red sun was almost gone beneath the horizon. Marveling at this city, he was, at the same time, frustrated by it. The worst part, of course, was that Bith was still locked in that trance. This whole thing was beginning to seem like a bad idea. He should be back in Westwood, fighting the minions of the Dark Lord, not moping around in an empty tower in a lost city.

And what use was this runesword of his in a place like this? There were no monsters to kill or dragons to slay. He pulled the blade from its sheath and ran his fingers along the runes. Where was the thrill he used to feel when he handled a runesword? He held the weapon by the hilt with two hands and waved it through the air, but it just made him feel worse. He sighed heavily.

There was a muffled noise from inside, then voices. Cal forgot his troubles and rushed to the others. Bith was back, cradled unsteadily between Hathor and Endril. She looked pale and weary, a shadow of the girl who had clutched the Stone that morning.

"Oh, my head," she complained. "It was so strange." Bith dropped the Stone back into the chest with a thump and rubbed her eyes. "I became another woman, a woman who lived in this city, but years ago. I lived her life, felt her feelings, and"—she frowned—"did her work!"

She rubbed her hands and arms, examining them carefully to be sure they were hers. She leaned over and glanced at her feet. There were her shoes.

"You know, the wildest part is that I can remember everything she knew, or had ever experienced in her lifetime." A look of awe spread over her face. "Yet, here I am, Bith again, with my own memories. My head is full of both of us. It is so odd."

"How do you know you were in the past and not just dreaming or something?" Cal asked.

Bith struggled to her feet. She was a bit wobbly, and Hathor steadied her. "Well, I think it was the past. I know it was the year three thousand and twelve as they reckon time around here."

"Means nothing to me—we haven't been here long enough to learn much," said the elf.

"Me either," added Hathor.

Cal just shrugged.

"Oh, another thing. I worked in the palace and I knew the caliph had a little dark-haired rascal of a son named Nabona."

"Could be. Every other caliph around this joint is named Nabona," suggested Cal. "Don'cha remember last night? It was some guy called Ibn an Nabona who got the city in trouble in the first place."

"Well, we'll find out soon enough." Bith smiled. "I don't know about either of you, but I've had a very hard day's work. I need a bath, and I'm starving. We can ponder the meaning of all this later."

CHAPTER
15
Trial and Error

That evening they dined with Nabona, and Bith related her mysterious adventure into the past. It was soon confirmed that she had indeed traveled back forty years to the time of the caliph's youth. He even remembered Mildred, for the woman had once chastised him for tracking across her clean floor with muddy shoes.

"Were I not such a kind and generous lad, I would have had her whipped for such impudence," Nabona said smugly.

Bith stirred, ready to make a scathing remark about the way he and his father treated their servants, then thought better of it. After all, such was the way of the world. The rich and powerful ruled and the poor served. She put her wineglass to her lips and took a long, thoughtful sip.

They were seated round a low table in a small room on the third floor of the palace, adjacent to a terrace. Through an open archway came a gentle summer breeze that rustled the long green fronds of the plants along the walls. Bith's mind drifted back to a moment she had experienced as Mildred, when the woman had stood outside the wall, staring into the haze, enjoying the sound of the wind in the trees.

"So how do you control that, er, Stone?" asked Nabona, breaking her train of thought. "How do you know to where or when you are going?"

"I was wondering the same thing myself," said Cal.

"If I knew that much," Bith said with a sigh, "I would probably have already accomplished our task. What took me into the body of Mildred is a mystery to me. But it is a mystery I intend to solve soon enough, I assure you."

"And what about the rest of us?" Cal asked. "Don't you think we should all hold the Stone and go back together? If we have to fight with the Dark Lord, it could be very dangerous. After all, we work best as a team."

"Well . . ." Bith was doubtful. "That's an interesting idea. However, I've yet to master the thing myself, and I'm a practiced magic-user. Granted, Endril has experience too, but you and Hathor have never dabbled in such things. With the rest of you involved, anything could happen. Let's wait and see."

The troll, who was clearly not at all interested in trying the stone, nodded. "Hathor glad to wait."

When she went to her bed, Bith's mind was filled with the new store of memories and experiences gained from being a part of Mildred. She also worried about the Stone and its possibilities. Could she learn to control it? And, if so, would she be able to go back in time to someplace besides the past of Abaton? And if that were possible, could she really alter events of the past to change the present?

She pulled the sheets up to her shoulders, certain she would lie awake all night, and then she promptly fell into a deep sleep. Mildred had been exhausted.

Hottar showed a snaggletoothed grin and grunted brusquely at the crowd of heavily armed giants. Some of them carried huge iron swords, others thick, two-bladed axes. The rest had massive spiked clubs slung over their shoulders. Over three hundred assorted giants from several clans crowded into the ruins of the recently captured hall. It was all that was left of a building that had once been a part of the city of Hamm, now lost to the Dark Lord. Smoking torches glowed red in the swirling mist and smoke that filled the area. It was early morning, but behind the Mistwall the light from the sun took a long time arriving. The giants had received their instructions and now were drinking the last of the wine from the cellars below, before marching off to battle.

Hottar, king of the frost giants, and designated leader appointed by Schlein, contemplated his army. Though few in number, three hundred giants were fully the equal of over six thousand armed men. He was confident that the forthcoming battle would be decided in favor of him and his kind. It bothered him little that he was serving the Dark Lord. Who, or whatever the Dark Lord was, Hottar had been well treated. His giants had been allowed to keep any and all spoils of battle, and the looting here in Hamm had richly rewarded his greedy band of giants.

He climbed atop an overturned bookcase and addressed his forces:

"To victory!" yelled Hottar, waving his mug of ale in the air. Hundreds of deep voices bellowed a thunderous cheer in reply, and hundreds of giants downed their drinks and threw the crocks in the general direction of the fireplace. The gesture nearly put out the great log fire, and more than one unlucky giant had a crock crash against his head or backside.

When the general uproar subsided, two tall doors swung open and the throng began to file out, following Hottar. Out they marched, into the iridescent swirling fog that was the Mistwall. It was half a day's march to the border of the unconquered lands and they had a long distance to cover.

As he trudged along the rocky trail in the murky half-light that passed for day behind the Mistwall, Hottar smiled to himself. Hill scouts had reported an unguarded pass in the mountains above the Kingdoms of the Westwoods.

He intended to march his army quickly into the heart of
Westwood, behind the enemy defenses, and come at his
foes from behind. A veritable work of genius for the dull
mind of a frost giant.

At the same time, several thousand trolls marched boldly
along what was once the main road between Castle Glencoe
and the now desolate city of Hamm. The troll army would
hold the attention of the defenders of Westwood while the
giants hit them by surprise from behind.

Bith had wanted to go alone to the dome at the top of
the tower, but her three companions would have none of it.
Cal, Hathor, and Endril insisted that they keep a vigil over
her while she worked with the Stone. As a compromise,
she persuaded them to watch over her in shifts, so that at
any given time only one of them would have to be present.
Endril was to use his free time poking around the city in
quest of magic of any form. If there were any magic-users,
or magic items of note, he was to bring them to Bith when
she returned.

As for Cal and Hathor, she insisted that the two take turns
on the training fields, honing their battle skills. She made it
quite clear that if the effort to change the past with the Stone
failed, their only hope of stopping the Dark Lord lay with
arms and armies.

They had flipped coins, and the troll drew the honor of
the first watch. Hathor sat against the wall now, with his
arms wrapped around his knees, watching Bith intently. By
his side was a fresh bucket of water and some towels. He
had insisted that a wet cloth had brought Bith out of her
trance before, and refused to let her begin unless he was
properly prepared.

Bith, who was seated on the couch, smiled at her loyal
friend. His eyes brightened and he returned her smile. She
swallowed the lump in the throat and opened the chest once
again, gently lifting out the Stone. The moment she touched
it, her fingers began to tingle with the powerful magic. Her

mind was still full of warm thoughts of gentle Hathor.

She lay back on the couch, but something made her keep her eyes fixed on the troll. He was still smiling. Bith experienced the familiar feeling of being in two places at once, then suddenly felt cold all over. Everything went black.

When she came to her senses, she was still cold. She opened her eyes and she felt a twinge of fear. All was still dark. Why was it dark? Had a day passed already? She called out to her friend. "Hathor, are you still there?"

A strange, reedy voice answered, "Yes, Mother!" A cold hand grasped hers reassuringly. Then a flood of memories washed over her, strange memories of a culture totally foreign to her own. Yet there was a common thread— a love for Hathor. Bith sat up with a jolt. Her son! The troll mother's muscular body tensed, and she reached out in the dark cave and pulled her son close to her.

Only she wasn't Bith, she was Gething, one of the many wives of Gemill of the Broken Fang. Bith probed the memories of Gething, shuddering at some of the gory details so common to the lives of hill trolls. There were many broken bones, and much blood, and chewed-on flesh. . . . Bith realized that Gething felt a similar revulsion to all these things, and suddenly knew how Hathor had come by his vegetarian ways. He had learned them from a nurturing mother, a mother who was proud of the way her son dared to be different.

She was about to speak, when a sense of imminent doom overwhelmed Gething. Bith knew that Gething had a sense which allowed her to see into the future. Her heart stopped. For Gething there was no future!

There was a sudden shriek at the end of the cave, and then the light of several torches flashed against the wet rock walls.

"Alarum! Alarum! Raider! Rai—ungh!" The voice was cut short in a death rattle.

"Quickly, my son." Gething led Hathor to the secret place, shoving the protesting young troll inside.

"Be silent, my dearest, if you value your life. They will not find you in here." She reached in one last time and ran her fingers through her son's hair. "Remember your mother loves you!" Gething rolled a boulder over the opening, then ran to her larder and pulled out a huge clay crock filled with blood. She dumped the contents over the floor, and trampled around in the muck a few times; that would throw their dogs off the scent. The torches were closer now. She dropped everything and ran for the back of the cave.

In her terror, she tripped over a tree stump. There should be no tree stump here! A torch flared in her eyes, and she was blinded. A gruff voice yelled out.

"Here's another!"

"Hold it down!" She caught a glimpse of an evil human face. Then saw and heard the axe as it hissed through the air toward her neck. Gething/Bith screamed at the top of her lungs!

Hathor stared silently at the beautiful form of Bith on the couch. He had been with her for over two years now, and at first she was more of a nuisance than a help. But that soon had changed, and the girl quickly proved her worth, as well as her greatness. Underneath the façade of ice was a sweet and gentle creature, a fragile thing of beauty. In fact, he guessed he loved her, in his own way. Somehow she reminded him of his mother, rest her soul. A single tear welled up in the corner of his eye, and he rubbed it away with his knuckle.

Just then, Bith fairly leaped off the couch, screaming— and headed for the balcony. Hathor jumped to his feet and grabbed her in the nick of time. She writhed and twisted in his arms, babbling incoherently, and to his amazement uttered several words in the troll language he had learned as a youth. Hathor muscled Bith back into the room and splashed water on her face. The effect was sudden, and the girl went limp.

Caltus had been in the courtyard below, teaching swordsmanship to one of the young noblemen who was next in line to leave the city. When he heard Bith's screams, he rushed to the tower, and there found the troll sitting beside the girl, holding her in his arms. She was sobbing violently.

"What on earth? What's wrong, Hathor?"

The troll shook his head. "She not say, just cry!"

"Bith! It's me, Cal!" She ignored him. The young warrior sat down on the other side of Bith, put his hand on her chin, and pointed her face at his. "Look into my eyes, Elizebith! Do you know who I am?"

The sobbing slowed to a few shudders and then came to an end. Hathor mopped up her tears with his damp cloth.

"Thanks . . . I" She looked at the troll and threw her arms around his neck. "Oh, Thor, we love you!"

Hathor rolled his eyes and looked sideways for help. Cal just shrugged and then smiled.

"This Stone is going to drive her crazy."

When Bith finally calmed down, she refused to explain what had transpired on her last trip. She was, however, insistent that Cal and Hathor leave immediately.

"I've figured out, I think, how to control the Stone, but with either one of you in the room, I'm liable to lose that control and venture back into some event from your past. And that isn't where I want to go!"

"But what about taking us with you?" demanded Cal. "You said you'd think about that!"

"Well, I have. And you can't possibly use this thing! And as for our traveling together, that's out of the question. The Stone is strictly a solo device. I meld myself with an individual from the past. One individual." She stood up on shaky legs and began to pace in circles around the couch. "Now, you two clear out of here so I can get some work done!" Bith began to babble theories of magic under her breath, seemingly oblivious to the other two.

Hathor looked at Cal. "She try to jump off balcony."

"Then we can't leave her alone!"

"Yes, you can," she interrupted. "Go get some wood and board up that door if you must. I have to do this in complete solitude."

"We talk to Endril first," said the troll. "This not good idea."

An hour later, after much argument, Hathor was finally persuaded to give into Bith. He brought up an old table, and with Cal's help, the balcony door was secured.

"Thank you. Please leave now," Bith said calmly.

Cal whispered to Hathor, "Maybe we should tie her down to the cou . . ."

"Out!" Bith glowered at them both.

"We're only doing this under protest," Cal said. Grudgingly, they locked the door at the top of the stair.

"Did you test the barricade, Thor?" The troll nodded. Neither Hathor nor Cal relished the thought of leaving Bith to her own devices. Reluctantly, they descended to the small, dark room below. It was as far away as they dared go, and they both intended to come running at the first sound of trouble.

Schlein pored over the open book that he held in his hand. Many other volumes lay scattered haphazardly around the stone floor. In came Griswold, a servant, with another pile of leather-bound tomes. He placed them timidly on the edge of the table and waited silently, hoping to catch his master's attention, yet not daring to speak. Griswold owed his long life to his keen awareness of Schlein's stormy moods, and of course to his iron constitution, which was strong enough to endure the worst physical abuse.

The wizard looked up impatiently. "Well, what is it?"

"Th-this is the last of them, Exalted Master. I have emptied the shelves." Griswold backed away slightly, ready to duck the blow that might come.

"Well, then," came the unexpected reply, "you can read, can't you?"

"Why, yes, Exalted Master."

"Then sit down on that bench and read!" Schlein pointed, and Griswold sat instantly. "Start with the red book on the top of the pile. I'm looking for any references to a place called Abaton!"

CHAPTER
16
Elissa

The two goblin sentries were leaning against a dead tree situated on a mountainside at the fringe of the Mistwall. Night had passed into morning, the fire was nearly out, and the goblins were half asleep. They probably wouldn't have noticed the three intruders if one of the men hadn't slipped on a patch of ice and fallen into the burning embers.

"Eeyow! Karkas, I'm burning!"

"Be quiet you fool," hissed a voice in the shadows. The noise wakened the dozing guards, and one of them jumped at the shadows.

"Who goes there?"

The other goblin unsheathed his sword and was instantly upon the man who had fallen into the fire. "Don't move or I'll slit yer neck!"

The man in the coals whimpered, but was still. The disturbance roused the rest of the sleeping goblins in the camp, and after a minor scuffle, all three of the men had been captured and bound with stiff ropes.

The goblin leader, who had taken his time entering the

fray, no doubt to be certain of the outcome, came striding up to the prisoners.

"Well, what've we here?" he snarled, absently picking his piglike nose with a dirty finger. "Spies from th' enemy camp down 'n th' valley, no doubt."

The three captives said nothing, so the goblin leader circled slowly around them and then drew a dagger. He pushed the tip of the blade against the shortest man's stomach. "What're ya doin' here . . . *spy*?"

The bearded man's eyes bulged with terror. "No! No!" he protested, "We—we're on your side, I uh, we all escaped from that camp. They, ah, they were holding us *prisoner* there!"

The goblin leader grinned. "Oh, ho! Yer with us, are ye? Well that's right interestin', considerin' you an' yer kind killed five o' my best soldiers t'other night."

"But—but, it's true," pleaded the man. "And we can reward you for—"

"Shut up, fool!" One of the other prisoners managed to knee the speaker in the groin, and the two fell to the ground in a heap.

The head goblin scratched his chin. "A reward, hey?" He signaled for help. "Search 'em from head to toe!"

The ensuing scramble, involving six greedy goblins and three unwilling captive men, resulted in the discovery of several pans, two plates, four spoons, and three gold bars, which one of the goblins held up triumphantly, greed gleaming in his red eyes. The leader instantly snatched up the treasure.

"Gimme those! So, yer gonna reward us?" He stared at the gold for a moment, then tucked the bars into his belt. "Snickvam, Sknurly, you two stay here and keep watch. The rest of ya bring these prisoners along. I think Snaefthg'll be interested 'n this."

Two torches were lit, and then the goblins marched the three miserable prisoners the short distance from the camp to the edge of the swirling Mistwall, and all disappeared within.

• • •

Endril finished the last line, written in a shaky hand on the final page of the small black book, and then carefully closed the worn cover. He refastened the leather thong with which it had been bound and handed the book back to the old man who had been watching over his shoulder.

"Thank you very much. It was exactly what I needed."

The man bowed silently as the elf walked out of the darkness of the musty library and into the light of day. He must return to the palace immediately and warn Bith of what he had learned.

Endril's search for magic in Abaton had met with little success. There simply were no magic shops or spellcasters to be found. What little magic was practiced in the city had been the province of the high priests, now long dead, and an occasional caliph.

His quest had finally led to the royal library, and the librarian had willingly shared the records of the caliph who had built the hall in which the Stone now resided. The book Endril had just finished reading told how the caliph had used the Stone to explore the past. The compelling paintings on the walls, those which Nabona had warned them not to look at, were records of the caliph's experiences using the Stone.

What worried Endril most was that the book also related the tale of how the Stone drained the life from the caliph and eventually drove him to madness. The last entry had been written by the royal physician after the man's death from old age. The old age of twenty-one!

Endril reached the palace and confronted Nabona with the information derived from the book.

"I warned you not to tamper with the Stone!" complained the caliph. "But that Elizebith was not to be denied. You know full well that I speak the truth."

"But the Stone will kill her!"

"Then I suggest that you and I, and your two other friends, try to stop her before it's too late."

• • •

Bith sat in the tower, alone, staring at the boarded-over door. Was that really necessary? Well, possibly. She knew that she had to use the Stone of Time again, to try to discover the beginnings of the Dark Lord, although how she could possibly alter his future reign of terror by some action of her own, she could not imagine. Her head and body still ached from the experience of being Gethring, and she knew somehow that the bone-deep weariness she felt was the result of having experienced death in another life.

She felt a deep empathy for the long-dead troll mother, and sorrow that her life had been taken when Hathor had been so young. Yet Thor had come out of it nicely. He was as kind and gentle as could be.

Bith shook the mood away. There was no time to feel pity for one who had been dead for decades. If she did not correct the problems of the present, her life would be forfeit just as Gethring's had been.

She clutched the Stone in her hand and stared at it without seeing, wondering, despite herself, what Gethring and young Hathor's life had been like. Had it always been hard and fraught with danger? Had Gethring enjoyed her childhood? Bith tried to call up the store of troll memories that mingled with her own. She called up the image of her own distant childhood and thought back on the person she had once been. Suddenly, she was seized with dizziness, a sense of things turning upside down, spinning, pulling her down, down, down, to be brought up sharply with a thump that knocked the breath from her body. She sat up slowly, regaining her breath, shook her head, opened her eyes and stared in utter shock!

She was sprawled out on a hillside dotted with fragrant highland flowers, red and blue and yellow and pink— groundsels, buttercups, wild roses, and gentians. Her mind identified them for her stunned senses. The hillside was thickly grown with deep green grass which she knew would reach halfway up her leg, caressing her like a lover's touch as she walked. These were her own memories!

And at the peak of the hill . . . Her eyes lifted and she saw as she knew she would, the great stone fortress that was the castle where she had spent her youngest years.

"Well, are you going to get up, or just lie there all day?" piped a snippity voice.

Bith turned on one elbow and found herself staring into a pair of silver eyes set into a narrow face with pouty lips and a pert pug nose. The face was framed with long black curls tied up in a handsome red bow. It was a face that she knew well, for it was her own. But if this was Bith, who was she? She looked down at her hands, and they appeared to be her own. Then a flood of memories came to her and she realized she was merged with yet another. She was the elf Sidonia, traveling east in search of her kin.

Bith touched her face and her elvish ears. They felt just the way they should. Yet something was different this time. Sidonia was a magic-user like herself. And . . . And she *knew* Bith was inside her! A chill of excitement ran down their spines. This realization was rudely interrupted.

"Speak up! Has the cat got your tongue?" a young girl demanded in an imperious tone. "This is *my* mountain and no one comes here unless I invite them. *You* are *not* invited!"

"Your mountain?" asked Bith/Sidonia, rising to her feet and dusting off her skirts. "How can a mountain belong to anyone but itself?"

"It *is* my mountain," said the girl, stamping her foot down an inch away from Bith's own, and staring up at her furiously. "You may *not* be here—you do not have my permission!" Her face began to grow red as her anger increased.

Bith stared at the unpleasant child. "But I am here, as you can plainly see," she said gently.

"Then I—I shall turn you into a toad!" cried the child.

"If you turn me into a toad, I shall grow into the very

largest toad in the world, and gobble you up," Bith said agreeably. "Although I think you would taste quite nasty." The words came to Bith's tongue as though she had said them before, and suddenly she realized why they were so familiar. She had heard them years ago as a child. She smiled at the unusual situation in which she found herself.

The child stared at her in amazement. "You can't do that," she said a bit uncertainly.

"Try it and find out," replied Sidonia.

"Well, get off my mountain," the child said petulantly, "Or I'll call my mother. Then you'll be sorry."

"And why should I be sorry?" asked Sidonia.

"Because my mother is Morea, the famous sorceress, and she can turn you into anything she wants with the flick of her fingers. Nobody is as good as my mother!"

"Do you really want to do that?" Bith/Sidonia asked gently. A shadow of something that might have been fear crossed the child's face. "No," she said softly. "No, I don't, but who are you and why are you here? No one ever comes here—they're too afraid. Aren't you afraid?"

There was a wistful tone in the child's voice, which struck to Bith's heart. She wanted to reach out and stroke the girl, hold her to her bosom, but she knew that she could not.

"It sounds like a lonely life," she said softly, crouching down so that she and the child were on a level. "Do you not wish for friends, companions to play with, someone to share your secrets with?"

The child's bright silver eyes stared into those of the elf maiden. "Your eyes . . ." she said in wonder, her voice faltering. Bith remembered the silver eyes of the elf she had met that day on the hill.

The little girl searched for words. "Lonely? Yes . . . I wish, I want . . ." Then she broke off and her back stiffened. She drew herself up tall and her eyes were sharp and glittered with suspicion. "No! I'm not lonely! Why should I be? I have everything I want. I do not need anyone but myself.

What do I need of playmates? And I keep my own secrets! Now leave. I do not like you and I want you to be gone!"

"As you wish," Bith/Sidonia said sadly as she began to walk down the hill. "But, my little friend, I'm afraid that we shall meet again one day whether you wish it or not."

The child stamped her foot again and began to tug at Bith's skirts. "What do you mean? Tell me what you know!"

Bith stared down at the child and pictured herself, fully grown. She wondered if her eyes looked that hateful, wondered if her voice took on that shrill, unpleasant tone. She was filled with sadness for the little girl who was herself, and the years of loneliness that lay ahead.

She had seen enough. Bith consciously willed herself back to the present, hoping she had the power. . . . There was the now familiar dizziness, and the strident voice of the child faded. She felt herself spinning, spinning, spinning. . . .

She clutched the stone and held it to her breast tightly, so tightly it hurt.

She did not need to open her eyes to know that she was back, that she had returned to her own time, to Abaton.

A knock on the door interrupted her reverie. It was Cal. "Bith, we heard you cry out. Is anything wrong?"

"No. No, everything is fine. I must go back again, now, please! I'll be all right. It's under control now."

Bith heard footsteps and voices disappear down the stairway. She felt a moment of sadness deep in her heart for the child that she had been. What little she could remember of her childhood had been surrounded by a mist of vague but pleasant feelings. Now, she could not help but wonder if they were true. Had she really been such a nasty, unhappy child?

Well she knew that Morea, her mother, that Mistress of Magic, had often twisted the past to suit her own purposes. Had she manipulated Bith's own memories as well? Morea was now in league with the Dark Lord. The beautiful mountain was gone forever. Rage as well as sorrow battled inside

Bith until she succeeded in thrusting them from her. Her mother was an issue that would have to be dealt with another day. For now, there were other, more pressing matters.

She started to rise, now wishing she hadn't dismissed her friends. She wanted to tell them what had transpired, but she was overcome with exhaustion and her legs felt weak and incapable of holding her. She sank down and pressed her hand to her breast, trying to regain her strength. Briefly, she wondered why she felt so exhausted every time she used the Stone.

As she sat there, holding the Stone, she was suddenly aware that she had grown quite accustomed to the tingling sensation that it produced in her hands and fingers. She pondered upon its magic and wondered just exactly how it worked.

She began to think about the nature of the task assigned to her by Geoffry and the coalition. How would she ever be able to find out how to stop the Mistwall? It was such an amorphous thing; her mind shied away from that dark image. Nor could she imagine discovering anything about the origins of the Dark Lord, for neither she nor anyone she knew had ever met that hideous master of evil. The memories of Sidonia flashed before her with sudden clarity. The elf she had been was fleeing the Dark Lord. Bith shivered.

There was only one person, one being who actually knew what was at the heart of the insidious plot. Only one person she could think of who was flesh and blood—Schlein. His image, hugely muscled, barrel-chested, blond and arrogant, came unbidden into her mind.

Against her conscious will she thought about him, holding his image firm in her mind's eyes, wondering what could have set him on the road to evil. Had he been born with a black nature? Was there ever a time when he had been good, or capable of being swayed to the side of right?

The swirling mists surrounded her once more, seizing her in their implacable grip and whirling her around and around. She began to feel cold.

"No," she cried silently. "Not again, not so soon. I am too tired." But the mists did not listen to her words, and she felt herself falling through time and space.

Once again she was lying on a flowered hillside, the thick grasses beneath her a fragrant carpet of green. But this time her head was cradled by caring arms, and she felt herself surrounded by an aura of love. Bith relaxed and savored the moment. She was not particularly anxious to open her eyes, or find out who and where she was.

Something feather-soft stroked her cheek. She opened her eyes and looked up into a handsome manly countenance. Blue eyes, filled with love and without a shadow of guile, looked into her own. "Are you happy, Elissa, love?"

Bith, who was now Elissa, examined her own thoughts and found that she was indeed happy. She loved this man, whoever he was . . . It was SCHLEIN! Bith's feelings of hatred and revulsion tried to surface, but they were overwhelmed by the emotions of the body she now inhabited.

Elissa raised her hand, slender and white and delicate, and caressed the thick blond tresses that hung to the man's muscular shoulders. She knotted her fingers in the heavy hair and tugged his face down toward hers, teasing his lips with her own, feeling his breath mingle with hers. She was consumed with love for this man, and hugged him to her to hide the flood of emotion that threatened to overwhelm her.

"Oh, my beloved," the man said in a ragged husky voice, gently withdrawing from her embrace. "There is nothing that I would not do for you. You shall have the world at your feet—this I promise. You shall want for nothing. I—Schlein, give you my word. You have but to ask and I will obey. You are my one true love, and I am yours to command to the very end of my days."

Bith fairly rejoiced. This was what she had been looking for. Schlein's past. A Schlein who was vulnerable. A

Schlein who would do anything for her! Elissa wrapped her arms around her lover's neck and drew him close, holding him tight. Caught up in the unbridled emotions she felt for this man, Bith/Elissa was unable to speak.

"I-I must leave you soon, my love," Schlein said, separating himself from her grasp.

Fear struck into Elissa's heart. "Why? Where are you going?" she asked, sitting up swiftly and staring at Schlein, who would not meet her eyes.

"Oh, nothing to concern yourself about, love. It's just some business I must take care of."

"What kind of business?" Elissa asked sternly, feeling her heart flutter in her breast. "The business of death, destruction, and pillage? And for that new menace from the west who calls himself the Dark One?"

"He is called the Dark Lord, and yes, perhaps what I will do involves killing," Schlein admitted with a shamed face. "But, my dear, that is what a man has to do sometimes. It's not pleasant, but someone has to do it. Don't bother your pretty little head about it. For just a few unpleasant acts, I shall be rewarded with a king's ransom. Then I'll be able to get you—"

She put her finger to his lips and silenced him.

"My darling Golden Bear," Elissa said with sorrow. "I beg you not to do this. Don't you understand that war and conquest are not forces of nature? They are not things that must happen like rain or snow or the change of seasons. War is the evil invention of man."

"Well, yes, there is that way of looking at it," Schlein said uncomfortably. "Yet, Elissa, you must admit that I have let you talk me out of numerous ventures in the past, which would have been quite lucrative." He sat up, a pained look on his face. "But this is something I must do, for the reward is too great to refuse. Besides, there are many, many repairs that I must make to Mother's castle, lest she suggest that she come and live with us after our marriage, and stonemasons do not come cheap."

Bith did not like the turn this conversation was taking. "Dearest Bear," Elissa said in her most charming voice, "your mother is more than welcome to come and live with us. Say that you will stay at home with me? Please?"

Schlein shuddered. "You do not know what you ask, my beloved. Mother come and live with us? No, a thousand times no. It cannot be. Nor will I let you sway me this time. It is only business that takes me away. There is nothing personal about it, and I promise to kill no more than I absolutely must. I must stand firm on this issue."

Elissa stared at the man to whom she was betrothed, and felt a deep sense of unease. "I-I don't know. There is something that troubles me. It is almost as though I can sense your death. Please don't go, beloved. I would die if I lost you."

Schlein laughed. "My death! What nonsense! What could possibly happen to me? And even if it did, which it won't why, your kisses can bring me back to life and then I would truly belong to you!"

"Don't joke about such matters!" Elissa said sharply. "I would rather you stayed at home than earn your love in such a way."

"You do not need to earn my love," replied Schlein. "It is yours for the taking. I would stay at home with you, my love, if I could, but I am bound by my word to attend to this matter. I have no choice. A man's word is his bond."

Elissa bowed her head, knowing that she could not sway Schlein in his decision. Once he made up his mind, it was final. She would keep watch over him as she always did when he was "away on business." The man was strong and noble and courageous or she would never have allowed herself to love him. But he seemed to surround himself with companions who did not share any of his qualities save strength. And they were eager to win him away from her, from what they saw as her ruinous charms. Every time they won, Elissa felt Schlein's love weaken. She was determined not to lose, but knew that it was a tricky game. She had to play her hand carefully, for if Schlein ever discovered that her goal was to wean him away from his companions and his "so called manly business," his pride and their love would suffer a mortal blow.

Nor could she allow him to learn that she kept watch over him during those times that he was away, and that her spells had often kept him from harm. He would not welcome the knowledge that her magic had kept him safe rather than his own skills and warrior's ability.

Bith was amazed at the means by which Elissa watched over Schlein, and smiled inwardly at the knowledge she was gaining from this woman—a thousand new spells she had never known, and many new ways to do old things.

Suddenly she felt cold again, and there was a pounding in her head. Bith opened her eyes to the dark room of the tower, just as the door opened and in came Endril, and the others, including Nabona.

The elf carried a lamp, and held it above the girl, who lay motionless on the couch. "Bith," he said gently, kneeling beside her and feeling her cheek. "Good, you're with us."

"I-I feel so tired."

Endril took the Stone from her hands and returned it to the chest. Her cheeks looked hollow, and there were streaks of grey in her long black hair. Nabona took the lamp, and her three friends carried her limp body back to the palace.

CHAPTER
17
Parting

Hathor held the mirror while Endril and Cal lifted Bith up so that she could see herself. They had carried her back to her bedroom. Bith looked in the glass, and her jaw dropped at the sight. She was years older than she had been just two days ago and there was a streak of grey in her hair!

"I'm sorry," apologized Endril, "but you must understand what using the Stone does to you. Now do you see how you have aged?"

Nabona made a *tsk tsk* noise from across the room, and shook his head. "It's my fault. I should never have given in and let you have access to it."

Hathor lovingly brushed her hair back out of her eyes, and Bith summoned what strength she could to sit up in her bed. She, too, was upset by the way she felt and what she had seen of herself. Yet she knew she had to continue. She was close, so very close, to what they had come here for.

"I know you all want me to stop this madness, but let me tell you what happened on my last trip. I saw Schlein in his youth. . . ."

Slowly she related the tale of Elissa and a much younger Schlein, and how the woman watched over the man and felt she could control him. Bith insisted that, with some help, she was certain she and Elissa could turn Schlein to the forces of good many years in the past. If that were so, the Dark Lord would lose his right hand, so to speak, and much of the evil that had befallen the world would simply not have taken place.

"Schlein make powerful ally," acknowledged the troll.

"What would happen to our past?" asked Cal, a puzzled look on his face. "Would the first battle of Cairngorm not have taken place? Would I have found the first runesword? Would we have come together at all?"

"You're missing an important point, all of you!" Endril was pacing back and forth. "To attempt this, Bith must use the Stone another time and drain herself even further."

"That is why we came here!" stated the girl flatly, "And that is what I intend to do."

Endril sat down on the bed beside Bith. "The book I read about the Stone never mentioned that the person wielding it could manipulate the past. At best, it will allow you simply to view things gone by."

"I must agree," added Nabona. "My father warned me about it when I was young. Do you not think that if we could alter the past, the caliphs of Abaton would have gone back and changed the awful sequence of events that led to our banishment?"

Bith disagreed, and they argued the matter a bit longer, till at last the girl fell sound asleep. The question of whether to continue with the Stone was tabled until morning.

Snaefthg, goblin king in command of the northern front, greedily contemplated the two gold bars that had been placed before him. It had been some time since he'd had any prospects of easy looting. His orders from Schlein had been specific. Advance on a broad front and overwhelm Roanwood. For a week now, all his efforts had met with bloody repulses at the hands of an extremely determined band of ogres.

The morale of his army had slumped to an all-time low. He was more than ready to give up on the seemingly pointless frontal assaults. Now, here was news of a great treasure, hidden almost under his very nose.

"You say the prisoners spoke of fabulous wealth stored in a cave not an hour's march from here?"

"Yes, Majesty."

The king held up a gold bar. "More of this just for the taking, eh?"

The messenger balked. "Well, not exactly. Before th' last of th' three died, he said somethin' about a treasure in a cave. Sngyx knows all about it."

Snaefthg nodded. A little looting would do his goblins good. He stuffed the gold into a pouch at his belt and rose from the camp table at which he had been seated.

"Call my captains. We march this morning, and not down the road again. This time we take the hills! Send Sngyx to me at once."

No one could stop Bith, and the next morning, barely able to walk, she made her way back to the tower, escorted by the others, who argued against what she was doing to the very last. Finally, she lay alone on the couch with the Stone.

Her thoughts drifted back to the sweet hillside where she had been Elissa. She felt suddenly dizzy. . . .

Elissa blinked and closed her eyes. When she opened them again, she was seated on the hillside. This time, however, she was alone. In her hands she held a milky globe veiled by clouds and mists that obscured whatever the globe held. She watched her crystal patiently, knowing that when the time was right she would be allowed to view that which she sought. Her heart was troubled, and her head throbbed and ached with a pain that had no source.

The globe cleared suddenly and Elissa saw a battlefield strewn with dead and dying, horses and men. The muddy ground was red with the blood that had been spilt. Lying in the center of the field, propped up on a mound of shields that had served as a futile rampart, was he whom her eyes had so anxiously sought. At first she thought that he was dead, for he was grievously wounded and his temple was black and bruised and streaked with blood. Then he moved.

What a fool he was, she thought to herself. She had taught him many spells, yet he still went into battle sword in hand. She brought the globe as close to her face as she could and studied the scene, trying to remain calm. Whether Schlein lived or died might well depend on what she did next. Bith considered an attempt to stop Elissa here and now. If she let Schlein die now . . . But the love Elissa felt was too powerful, and it infected Bith. She was a powerless witness to what was about to transpire. Endril had been right.

An arrow had pierced Schlein's shoulder, but it had passed through the thickest portion of the muscle and the wound would heal, leaving little more than a puckered bit of flesh. He had taken a sword thrust through the calf of his leg and through his side as well. The head injury was nasty, but not critical. It was the wound in his side that was the most dangerous, for it had pierced something vital inside him and he was bleeding from within. Elissa knew that not even the best of healers could stanch internal bleeding. If Schlein were to be saved, she would have to do it, and it could not be done from afar.

Elissa bit her lip, wondering what to do, although she knew there was no real question. She would do what she had to do and then pray that he was strong enough to face the fact that a woman had saved him.

Elissa gathered the items that she needed—a bird's feather, the membrane from a bat's wing, some nightshade to ease the pain, and a cloak of darkness to conceal their passage. Bith tried to make mental notes, then realized it wasn't necessary: she would remember all this when she awoke.

Elissa placed the cloak around her shoulders, held her bag of magic items in one hand and the globe in the other, then said the words that would take her to the side of the man she so dearly loved. She closed her eyes.

The transition was smooth as always. One minute she was standing on the flowered hillside with soft breezes playing with the curls around her cheeks. The next, she was standing in the middle of a bloody field with the cries of the dying ringing in her ears. But she had no eyes for anyone other than Schlein. Now that she was actually there beside him, his wounds seemed far more grievous than they had appeared in the globe. Blood had pooled beneath him and he was very weak, barely able to open his eyes and whisper her name when she gathered him to her.

She wasted no time in speaking, other than making meaningless murmurs of comfort, for there was much to be done. With shaking fingers, she crumbled the nightshade and mixed it with a bit of water and other powders tapped from a tiny vial. This she held to Schlein's bloodless lips. Schlein swallowed the mixture in silence, his eyes closed. Some of the fluid dribbled out the side of his mouth. Elissa was terrified that he would die before she was able to heal him.

She forced herself to let go of him, allowing him to fall back against her legs, freeing her hands so that she could fumble in her pouch for the necessary ingredients while she struggled to bring the words to mind. They eluded her and she struggled to control her frazzled nerves. Finally, she calmed, and was able to bring the words into focus. She said them, wondering if it was too late, for it seemed that the life had drained out of Schlein.

For a moment nothing happened and she feared that she had failed. Tears slipped from beneath her lids and fell upon the recumbent form—tears not just from Elissa but from Elizebith as well.

"Why are you crying, beloved?" Schlein whispered. Elissa opened her eyes, and through her tears, saw Schlein staring up at her, his eyes as blue as the sky above their flowered hill.

"I-I feared you were dead," whispered Elissa. "I feared I was too late to save you," she said, knowing even as the words escaped her lips that they were more dangerous than any arrow, wishing that she could call them back.

"Save me?" Schlein said with a frown, rising up onto his elbow. He looked around him, seeing, and then remembering, where he was and what had happened to him. He touched the scar on his shoulder where moments before the broken shaft of an arrow had protruded. He touched his temple gingerly and stared at his fingers which came away unstained by blood. "How? Where did you come from? What has happened here?"

"Do you not know, Schlein?" came a gravelly whisper. Schlein turned to the side, and Elissa, following his gaze, started in horror as she saw a bloody figure rise from the ground and grip Schlein's arm with a mangled hand. It was Garix, the worst of Schlein's boon companions. A filthy man who had always viewed her as the enemy and seldom missed the opportunity to slip in an evil word.

Garix resented their betrothal and every minute that he was deprived of Schlein's company. To his mind, drinking and warfare were far and away more worthy of a 'real' man's attention. He had all but convinced Schlein that sorcery was not something that 'real' women involved themselves in. According to Garix, 'real' women stayed at home tending the children and the cooking and the chores, and left magic and other important matters to their menfolk.

When he was alone with Elissa, Schlein could close his ears to Garix's viperous talk, but all too often he was swayed by those thoughts, for they were prevalent among most of his rowdy, none-too-intelligent companions.

"Can you not guess?" whispered Garix as a dribble of blood fell from his nostrils, staining his scraggly mustache.

"She has used her wiles on you, practiced her magic, and saved your life. Did you not feel her holding your hand throughout the battle?"

"Elissa would not do that," said Schlein. A worried look crossed his face.

"She is a meddlesome witch. The battle has gone against us, a battle we should have won. All of us are dead, all of us save you. Why have you alone been spared, Schlein? Think on it when you lie in her arms. Think about betrayal."

Garix coughed, and a great gout of blood poured from his throat. His eyes rolled back in his head and he fell against Schlein, dead.

Elissa could not meet Schlein's eyes. The sounds of battle were growing louder. She gripped the bird's feather and muttered the words to another spell as she spread the cloak around them both. Clouds swirled, time sped past, and then they were seated on their hillside once again.

Somehow, Garix was there too, sprawled gruesomely on the beautiful hill, even uglier in death than in life.

"You promised that you had given up this nonsense," said Schlein.

"Is it nonsense that I have saved your life?" asked Elissa.

"My life did not need saving," said Schlein. "I can take care of myself."

"I saw you!" cried Elissa. "You were dying!"

"Were you spying on me?" yelled Schlein.

"Spying?" Elissa's voice cracked. "Spying? Is that what you call it? I was keeping watch over you because I love you! If that is what you call spying, you are a bigger fool than I ever thought possible!"

The two of them stared at each other, hateful words on their lips and agony in their hearts. They heard themselves say words they did not mean, felt the pain on tender hearts and fragile egos, and were too young and proud to know how to undo the damage they were inflicting. Bith could not believe what had transpired. All the confidence seemed to have gone from Elissa. She was totally defeated.

Schlein struggled to his feet. "See me no more! I owe you my life, and for that I thank you." He looked down at the hideous corpse of his dear friend Garix, then turned his back on Elissa.

And when they parted, each walking stiffly in opposite directions, each yearning to hear the other call his name, take back the hateful words, they heard nothing but silence.

Bith awoke on the couch, filled with despair. Neither she nor Elissa had been able to change a thing. Schlein was bent on a life of service to the Dark Lord.

Bramble sat by his fire all that first day after the intruders left, and contemplated the Arthana thing, which the girl had said would protect him. Against what, he was not sure. He was smarter than the occasional wolf or bear that wandered his way. And the treasure seekers, they always went into the cave and never returned . . . until now. Still he was worried. The Arthana had never stayed this close to him before.

By the second day, Bramble was positively starving. He had eaten all the food the people had given him, yet he was afraid to leave with the Arthana so close by. He began to dream of a nice roast rabbit, and was shocked when the thing came to life and began to walk toward the entrance of the cave.

Minutes later, Bramble was further surprised, when the Arthana returned, carrying a freshly killed rabbit in its metal claw. It dropped the meal at the hermit's feet and fell silent. From that moment on, Bramble changed his mind about the Arthana.

He learned, through trial and error, that he could will the metal thing to do his bidding, and soon the Arthana was bringing food on a daily basis, even fetching water in a pan from the creek. Bramble was beside himself with joy. Never in his long life in the cave, had he enjoyed such luxury.

One afternoon, however, as he watched his new servant rattle back up the hill with its load of water, Bramble caught a movement out of the corner of his eye. A movement where there should be none. He crouched low and made his way stealthily back to the cave. Whatever was out there, he did not want to be seen. He was relieved when the Arthana finally came clanking through the entrance and fell silent.

The hermit did not have long to wait. On the heels of his Arthana came three pig-faced goblins, one carrying a lighted torch. Bramble froze in the shadows. The goblins glanced nervously from side to side and then signaled others. Soon the cave had filled with the smelly creatures, milling about and poking into Bramble's precious hoard of blankets and cutlery. Panic filled his heart, but there were too many of them for him to do . . . Wait a minute! The Arthana!

Just then a pompous figure pushed his way into the cave, and the others ducked away before him.

"Sngyx, which way is this tunnel?"

"Back here, my king. The rock is not what it would seem."

The goblins marched through the wall of illusion and into the back of the cave. More poured in through the entrance and Bramble's eyes bulged with disbelief. He should have been discovered long ago, and the goblins completely ignored the Arthana.

He puzzled for a moment. More magic. He didn't know how it worked, but was pleased to still be alive. The procession of goblins continued. He tried counting, but lost track after three hundred had passed by. Finally the entrance was empty. Bramble shook his head and crept forward. What would he do when they returned?

Just then the Arthana came to life. Two metal claws came out through small doors in its side, and it marched slowly and methodically through the wall of illusion into the tunnel behind. Bramble smiled when he heard the screams. He knew he would have no further trouble with the fools who had marched into his cave. He gathered up his blankets and was soon sound asleep.

CHAPTER
18
The Woman in the Shadow

"Hand me the pen, Endril."

The elf complied, and Bith scribbled a date on the bit of paper she had placed on the table. She looked up at the others. "With this, I hope to be able to pinpoint a specific time, as well as a specific person and place for my next . . ."

"And last!" insisted Endril.

"And last," she continued, hoping her lie could not be discerned, "trip back in time." Bith knew full well that what she intended required her using the Stone at least two more times. She hoped her constitution was up to the wear and tear it was going to receive. "When I return, I will, I hope, have an idea what Schlein has in mind for us all. Even if I cannot alter the past, we can use the information I garner to change the future."

That line of logic had been the only reason Endril had agreed to this further experiment with the Stone.

Just then the door burst open, and a breathless messenger ran over to Nabona and whispered in his ear. The caliph's eyes opened wide.

"Well, it seems that others have found their way to our fair city. I must attend to this at once. Do let me know if the young lady's trip meets with success." He stormed out the door with his robes flapping behind him.

Bith could see the curious looks on the faces of her companions. "I'll be safe enough up there alone. You go with him and see who it is."

"I'll wager ten to one it's Schlein," said Cal.

Endril nodded in agreement. "You and Hathor go on. If it is Schlein, there will be need of that runesword. I'll see Bith safely to the tower and then join you."

A hurried trip took them to the top of the stairs.

"Be careful," said Endril, locking the door.

Elizebith clutched the Stone and closed her eyes. She could feel the magic surge through her body. In her mind she formed a mental image of Schlein, while on another level she struggled to concentrate on the date she had written on the bit of paper. For a moment all was silent, then cold. Suddenly she felt the now familiar rush of transferral, followed by the shock of coexisting with another being.

She rubbed her eyes and then opened them, and there was Schlein, seated at the end of the table. A chill went down Bith's spine. A chill shared by the woman whose body she now occupied. The memories came to her, and Bith knew who she was. She was now sharing the life of Zendra, Queen of the Black Valley Tribes. Zendra was not at all pleased with what the Dark Lord's captain, Schlein, had to say. He had just appointed a frost giant and an incompetent witch to command. She would be damned in hell before she, Zendra, would take any orders from that worthless Thidluke, or that dimwit of a giant, Hottar.

Bith was startled as she looked down at her/Zendra's hands, which were clutched tightly on the table before her. Her skin! It was a mottled blue! Then the memories of Zendra filled in the gaps and Bith was again at ease. Woad, of course. The leaders of this tribe had painted themselves with the blue dye for as long as she could remember. It was a sign of distinction, as well as one of power, and the magic properties instilled by the dye were limitless.

Zendra tried hard not to listen to the plans as they unfolded, for she was to be but a follower. Bith, however, fought hard to overcome the indifference and listened as carefully as she could. They were planning the overthrow of Westwood, and Glencoe itself!

Bith congratulated herself on her skillful use of the Stone. This conference, or something like it, was exactly what she had been seeking! With all her powers, she managed to exclude the hateful and distracting things that Zendra was thinking and, with difficulty, followed most of the conversations at the table. Schlein left abruptly, and the frost giant took charge of the conference, much to Zendra's distaste.

The session lasted for over an hour, and Bith was not sure just how valuable what she had overheard would be to Geoffry. Disappointment began to set in. She had advance information of an attack, but Westwood was expecting an attack anyway. Just then, Hottar stood and proudly announced his plan. The trolls grumbled. His giants would march secretly through Eagle Claw Pass, which was unguarded, and take Glencoe from the rear. Bith's ears pricked up. At last!

Zendra, however, would not cooperate. She began making obscene noises and ridiculing the giant. The trolls began to snigger among themselves, and Hottar took offense. He unslung his great axe, and brought it crashing down on the table, cleaving it neatly in half. As splinters, and bits of plates, bottles, and conference attendees, flew in every direction, Bith lost her grip, and awoke in Abaton with a start.

There was a banging on the door. It opened, and in rushed Endril with a lamp.

"Quickly, Bith. You must give it up!" he said breathlessly. "The forces of the Dark Lord have somehow found us. The city is under attack. We must have your assistance or all will be lost!"

Bith rose shakily to her feet, then reconsidered. "Not yet, Endril. There is one final journey I must take with the Stone, before I can come."

The elf grabbed her by the shoulder, ready to drag her out by force if necessary. "I tell you Bith, there is no time left!"

She glared into his eyes, and he froze. "Listen to me, Endril. I have wasted days here with this damned artifact and have accomplished next to nothing, except to make myself older. I've found no sign of the Dark Lord's mysterious past, and I was unable to alter Schlein's evil ways. Now, at last, I have stumbled onto something valuable. There is a way I can put it to good use." She put her hand on his shoulder and softened. "I'm going back one more time, right now. Go, use your powers to fight them. I will be with you soon." She pointed out the door.

Endril wavered for a moment, torn between leaving her here alone with the city under attack, yet unable to resist her newfound power of command. She was using a magic on him now that he had never before experienced. Whatever else this Stone had done, it had certainly matured Bith far beyond her years. He turned and made for the door, then stopped, looking back.

"Please hurry," he said and then he was gone.

Cal led the way up the stairs ahead of Hathor, and they came out on the crowded parapet above the North Gate of the city. Nabona was there among the throng of soldiers and citizens who had climbed the walls. Cal was shocked by the vision spread out before them.

There in the purple haze that perpetually surrounded Abaton was a swirling snakelike cloud that seemed to be boring its way through the haze and establishing itself firmly to the ground not fifty feet from the wall. Cal knew in an instant what it was, and he shuddered. Hathor recognized the swirling tornado as well.

"Mistwall!" the troll exclaimed.

"Damn!" yelled Cal. Then he turned to the caliph, who was staring spellbound at the pulsating, intruding cloud. It had grown visibly larger, and a black opening appeared in its side, just above ground level.

"Nabona, listen to me. That thing is evil! Call out your soldiers at once. The Dark Lord has followed us here! You are under attack."

"What? Impossible! We have never—" As he spoke, the throng on top of the wall let out a low cry. Out of the black hole in the side of the tunnel of Mistwall emerged a huge grey figure that appeared to be made of stone. It stood nearly as tall as the city wall. Its head resembled a rough hewn boulder and its eyes were deep-set black pits. It walked stiffly on massive legs, one slow step at a time, toward the gate.

"Stone golem," whispered Hathor. "Bring runesword," said the troll, hefting his axe over his shoulder.

"Open the gate," yelled Cal. "We're going out! And get some soldiers up here, fast!" The two made their way quickly down the way they had come.

The gate swung open for a moment and the two advanced on the stone monstrosity that towered above them. The golem paid Cal and Hathor no mind and inched its way toward the gate tower. Hathor swung his axe in a circle over his head and charged at one of the monster's thick legs. There was a ring of steel, and a fist-sized hunk of stone flew off and bounced against the wall.

Cal followed slowly, unsheathing his runesword and advancing, possibly more cautiously than he should have. Something was wrong. A runesword had always filled him with the fire and fury of battle. He should have been consumed with blood lust, yet he found himself plotting carefully for a single blow, and worrying lest he damage the fine edge on the blade.

Meanwhile, Hathor had hacked out another hunk of the great stone leg. The golem, still ignoring its attacker, brought its great stone fist down upon the crowded gallery atop the gate, breaking away a large section of the masonry, as well as smashing two hapless onlookers to screaming deaths.

Cal swallowed hard, whirled the blade over his head, and slashed at the ankle of the same leg Hathor was relentlessly attacking. He had no knowledge of golems, but if this thing had an Achilles' heel, this would surely cut it. Sword struck stone with a fearsome ring, and the shock of the impact shuddered through Cal's limbs. His hands and arms went numb and he winced violently, closing his eyes for a second.

When he opened them, he could see half his blade spinning off into the distance. There was but a stump left beyond the hilt still in his hands. Before he could let out the string of oaths that came instantly to his mind, Hathor grabbed him by the sleeve and pulled him backward, just in the nick of time. Cal's sword-breaking blow had indeed severed the leg of the stone monster, and, having lost its balance, the massive thing was falling like a giant tree— in their direction.

"Run!" yelled the troll.

The golem crashed to the ground, smashed into a pile of rubble, and collapsed. A hunk of rock flew up and glanced off Cal's forehead, knocking him to the ground. All went black.

Bith scrawled a diagram on the dust on the floor by the couch. It was just barely visible in the dim light of the lamp, but there was no time to go fetch pen and paper. She picked up the Stone and concentrated on the small room she had been in once before. Up the spiral stair in Castle Glencoe . . .

This time, she would not go to the past, but just slightly to the future. Bith hoped and prayed that the difference would allow her an ability she had been denied in her previous trips. She suddenly felt cold, and then awoke with a start.

Opening her eyes, she was surprised to see a long, flowing white beard hanging off the end of her chin and a mustache that tickled her nose. An old, bony hand reached up and stroked the beard. She was with Greenlock! Bith ignored the flood of the old man's memories as they surged into her mind. No time for that. She struggled with all her might to gain control of the hand that was twisting at the beard.

Greenlock shuddered. What had come over him? What in blazes was wrong with his hand? Too much to drink last night, maybe? Bith screamed in his mind: *NO, you old fool! Write what I have to tell you!*

The old wizard shook his head and frowned, then reached automatically for the pen and ink on the corner of his table. His hand, propelled by a force he did not understand, began writing swiftly across the blank page of a book. He stared in amazement. It was not in his hand.

When the message was finished, and signed "Elizebith of Morea," he understood. Greenlock grabbed the paper and ran out the door.

Bith sighed and let the Stone roll from her body to the floor. She was back in the tower. For a moment she couldn't move. Then she forced herself to her feet, and staggered down the stairway to the small room just inside the hall of pictures. She opened the door and stepped out, and was shocked to find herself face to face with an old woman.

In the dim light she could barely make out the features of this woman, yet there was something strangely familiar about her. Bith looked into her eyes and recognized her at once—it was Elissa.

"I knew you would come!" said the old woman.

"How? How did you know? How did you come here?" stammered Bith.

Elissa smiled. "I did not give up on him. I have been here for years, using the Stone in secret. Someday . . ." Her voice trailed off. "But now you must take action. He is coming to destroy us and you are our only hope!"

Elissa took Bith's hand and placed a small, soft object in her palm. "This is a powerful charm. You will know when to use it!"

Bith looked at it. It was a lock of red hair.

"Who is coming, who is going to destroy us?" pleaded Bith. But in her heart she knew the answer. Elissa disappeared into the shadows without a word. Bith called after her, but there was no answer.

Moorlock stood beside Philemus in the tower and watched the rider hurry along the road through the trees. He sensed that this was something important and nudged his companion.

"See that," he said, pointing at the horse and rider approaching the camp. "It will be important. Let us meet him halfway."

The two descended the series of ladders and made their way to the log cabin below, where a fire burned cheerfully in the center of the floor. Several sentries huddled around it for warmth. Just as Moorlock and Philemus entered, the courier burst through the door.

"Milord," he cried, spying Moorlock across the room. "An urgent message from the king." He handed the young prince the message so recently written in Bith's hand by Greenlock.

"Ha!" uttered Moorlock, handing the note to Philemus. "We've not a moment to lose! Sergeant, summon the nobles immediately."

Trumpets blared, and there was a flurry of activity. Men came rushing out of tents, cabins, and lean-tos. The leaders of the army assembled around a table, with Moorlock at the head.

Moorlock spoke. "Men, we have just received a vital piece of information from the four heroes." He held up the paper. "We have here the enemy's plan of attack." There was a general growl of approval. "There is a troll army advancing down the main road. Their objective is our position here, but theirs will not be the real assault. Our wall should be sufficient."

Moorlock leaned over the map and pointed. "Here, Eagle Claw Pass—" He looked sideways at one of the nobles. "Lord Currock, you declared it impassable this time of year."

The man cleared his throat uneasily. "But it . . ."

"No matter. There'll be a force of giants coming through there tomorrow. It will be up to us to arrive first and lie in ambush."

Further plans were made as to how to deal with the troll onslaught. Philemus and Moorlock were to lead the best of the troops up the rocky path that led to the pass, where they would lie in wait for the unsuspecting giants.

An hour after the note had arrived, Moorlock and Philemus rode out at the head of a column of five hundred of Glencoe's finest soldiers. Half of them were archers, the rest men-at-arms. Far out in front, two dwarfs, miners who lived in these mountains, were scouting the trail, in search of the best place to lay the trap.

The ride was long and difficult, and by nightfall the trail was so steep that the horses were left behind. A small group of grudging volunteers had to take them back to the main camp in the valley below. None wanted to miss the big fight at the pass.

The first light of dawn found the rock faces above Eagle Claw Pass lined with archers. Down below, Philemus positioned the men-at-arms strategically behind boulders and clumps of short pine trees.

There was no sun that day, and the giants, confident that their attack would be a surprise, strode along noisily, failing to send out even a single scout. The men of Glencoe remained silent as the ranks of the enemy marched clumsily past. Twice, giants walked behind trees to relieve themselves and nearly discovered the danger into which they were blundering.

At last, near noon, a single shrill trumpet sounded, and a shower of deadly arrows fell to their marks. Men wielding pole arms surged in to mop up the survivors, who were many, for giants are not easy to kill. Hottar's minions fought valiantly despite arrows protruding from their bodies like quills on a hedgehog. The frost-giant king rallied what he could of his forces in a box canyon and charged the attacking forces.

All afternoon the battle of the pass raged, and by nightfall it was over. A giant might be the equal of twenty men on open ground, but in the confines of the narrow mountain defile, the men of Glencoe proved their worth. It was said that only two of the giants escaped, those being the cowards who fled at the first sign of trouble. The rest were dead. Along with them perished the cream of the army of Glencoe.

The next evening, a ragged band of but forty men staggered back to camp. The bodies of Moorlock and Philemus, both of whom had died valiantly in the battle, lay in state for all to see.

While the battle of the pass had raged, the troll army had been repulsed at the wall. Beyond the Mistwall, the wode-painted tribes led by Zendra—for Thidluke was mysteriously absent—had deserted the cause and returned to their lands without a fight. All along the line, the forces of the Dark Lord had been turned away, and Glencoe had been saved. The Mistwall was moving west, back in the direction from which it had come.

Farther north, Govorn and his ogres, who guarded Roanwood, marveled when morning came and they stared across their barricade. Where once the Mistwall had loomed ominously close, just beyond their fragile defense, there was now clear grey sky. The dreaded cloud was nowhere to be seen.

CHAPTER
19
Schlein's Moment

The doors to the gate swung momentarily open, and out dashed three men who helped Hathor gather up the unconscious Cal and drag him back inside the walls. Soon thereafter, goblins by the hundreds began to emerge from the black hole in the side of the sinuous, evil shape that pierced the haze.

The goblins marched left and right in neat ranks, swordsmen with shields closest to the walls, and archers behind them. The forces of evil deployed in two long rows on either side of the gate, but did not fire any shots in anger.

Nabona, meanwhile, had not been idle. Many of the women and children were evacuated to the safety of the palace. The great arms cache, not opened since the city had been set adrift in time, was opened. From the palace streamed a steady line of defenders, both male and female, to take their places on the walls. They were wearing armor which had not seen the light of day for centuries.

Endril had returned and examined Cal's wound. The young warrior had come around, but was still a bit groggy.

"That's quite a lump you have on your head!"

Cal groaned. "That's nothing. Did you see what happened to my runesword?"

Hathor held up the remaining portion of the broken sword.

"Didn't last very long this time, did it?"

"Hey! This is no laughing matter." Cal rubbed his swollen forehead. "If I get my hands on that Vili . . ."

There was a noise outside the wall like a clap of thunder. Hathor helped Cal to his feet and the three climbed back up the wall to see what was going on.

They took their places beside Nabona, who was wearing a suite of polished bronze armor. Out beyond the wall, near the swirling vortex of the portion of the Mistwall that had come to Abaton, glowed a brilliant fireball. All on the wall were forced to shade their eyes.

The flames began to dissipate, and there was a puff of black smoke. Out of the vapor stepped Schlein. He put his hands on his lips, surveyed the broken golem, and then stared up at the top of the gate tower.

Bith arrived and stood beside her friends. Cal put his arm around her, and Endril and Hathor patted her gently on the back.

Schlein spied the foursome and grinned.

"Elizebith, you and your friends just don't know how much trouble you have caused me."

More goblins began to file out of the black hole behind Schlein and line up behind the others.

"You there in the silly armor," said Schlein, addressing Nabona. "You seem to be a reasonable man. I have no quarrel with you or your people. I came here for two reasons." He walked forward a few paces. "Give me the Stone of Time . . . and those four. Give them to me, and perhaps we won't destroy this miserable excuse for a city."

Nabona stood up on a chair and yelled back defiantly. "Certainly, you may have them all"—he paused dramatically—"over the dead bodies of every man, woman, and child in this city!"

The forces on the wall broke into a rowdy cheer.

Schlein shrugged and shook his head sadly. When the noise subsided, he yelled, "I'm going to enjoy this more than I thought I would!" He signaled to the goblin leaders, then rubbed his hands together in anticipation.

The goblins tensed, and bows were drawn.

Bith stepped up to the wall and called out, "Wait!" She turned to Nabona. "Open the gate and let me out there." Before any of her friends could stop her, the girl was down the stairs and out on the road confronting Schlein.

"Well, what is this?" he asked with a snarl.

Bith pulled out the charm given her by Elissa and held it in plain view against her breast. Tears began to stream down her eyes, as she felt the pain Elissa had experienced when Schlein left her. To the amazement of all, Bith changed and became Elissa in appearance. Flaming red hair and all, she was the Elissa of old—the Elissa from Schlein's deep dark past. All fell silent, even the goblins.

She took a step forward and reached out to him. "My darling Golden Bear, has it come to this?"

Without speaking, the great bulk of Schlein shuddered visibly, and he held out his massive arms and signaled the goblins. They put down their arms.

"W-What did you say?" Schlein's eyes widened and soon were filled with tears as a flood of old sweet memories was unlocked from the recesses of his ice-cold heart.

The girl's lips trembled and she spoke softly. "I said, spare us now, my darling Golden Bear!"

He walked slowly forward and touched her cheek. "You once saved me from death, dear one. I owe you this much at least." Schlein turned on his heel and gestured to the black hole. Posthaste, the goblin troops began swarming back whence they had come.

Minutes later, they had all gone, and Schlein alone stood before the wall. Then he too vanished in a ball of flame, as he had come.

The gates to the city flew open and a crowd of admirers swept around Bith. She had by now returned to her normal state, and Hathor, Cal, and Endril lifted her on to their shoulders, and the girl was marched triumphantly back to the palace.

The four heroes, now heroes of Abaton as well as many other places, stood on the balcony to the cheers of the populace below. Each time Nabona raised his hand, they would cheer louder than before. Eventually the people were quiet, and Nabona made a long-winded speech to the citizens, introducing, one at a time, the three brave men of the city, who with their caliph were about to leave Abaton in quest of the outside world.

"We have no way of knowing for sure whether we shall return. But this time—this time I think our chances are very good, for we have the help of the greatest sorceress of all time, Elizebith of Morea!" Another wild roar came from the crowd, and people threw hats and flowers into the air. At a signal, a flock of white pigeons was released, and they fluttered noisily skyward, darting first one way and then another.

That afternoon, the people lined the streets and stood on the walls, watching, hoping, and praying, as the four heroes, accompanied by four of Abaton's own, mounted their horses and rode out the north gate. Down the road they went and into the purple haze, and then they were gone.

Within the city of Abaton, no one moved. At each gate there was an anxious crowd of people, each of whom hoped to be the first to see the return of their men. They waited patiently; sunset was the appointed hour. As the sky grew dark, some of the skeptics turned and began to walk away.

Then, from the south wall, a cheer went up, and was swiftly taken up by all the citizens. The bells of the city began to ring, and they would ring for a long time to come, for men had left the city and returned that day. Abaton, in its own strange way, had reestablished its ties with the rest of the world.

It was dark now, and the four rode down a lonely road. In the distance they could see a small village and they urged their mounts forward. Bith shivered, pulling her cloak about her shoulders.

"I had forgotten how cold it was. I guess I was spoiled by the summer of Abaton."

"It had it's good points," said Cal.

"Best roots ever," joked Hathor. He had a bag full of two-foot tubers hanging from his saddle.

"In all, I would say we've done well," remarked Endril. "But we still have some fighting to do when we return."

"Maybe Bith's message was in time," suggested Cal. "Maybe those giants were whipped."

"Hope so," commented the troll.

They passed into a wood and Endril brought them to a stop. "Listen, did you hear that?"

Bith frowned. A strange voice was chanting to them from somewhere among the trees.

"Calloo Calee, you there beneath yon tree!"

They all recognized the voice instantly.

"Amys and Amylion! It's Gunnar Greybeard!" exclaimed Cal. Now they could see a fire burning in the glade, and by it stood a wrinkled dwarf with a grey beard. Atop his head was a pointed red cap, and he waved happily at the four.

"Come, my friends and join me round the fire." Even Bith, who never quite approved of Gunnar, was glad to see him, for his fire was cheery and he always had plenty of good food and drink.

Later, as they sat remembering old times, Gunnar mentioned the reason he had been sent to find them.

"Vili sent you again?" Bith asked.

"Yes, of course," replied the dwarf. "You see, there's the matter of yet another runesword to be retrieved."

"Not worth the effort," yelled Cal angrily, jumping to his feet. He went to his saddlebags and produced what remained of the sword he had taken from Arthana's cave. "This was the best Vili himself had to offer us!"

Gunnar took the broken sword, looked at it briefly, and then tossed it into the fire. It melted away like so much frozen water.

"Hey!"

"It's a fake!" said the dwarf calmly. "Look, I have some good news and some bad news. What would you like first?"

The four looked to one another. Cal spoke. "The good news, I guess."

"All right, I've just come from Castle Glencoe. The Dark Lord has been defeated on all fronts, thanks mostly, I hear, to what you four have done. You are quite the heroes, you know."

Bith was all smiles.

"And the bad news?" asked Cal timidly.

"Well, Vili went to this big bash they were giving back in Valhalla and he ran into Loki. Seems the old fox heard about you folks and decided to play a trick on you."

"What?"

"That wasn't Vili who met you on the road, it was Loki. And the sword you carried was just a piece of junk!"

"I might have known." Cal slapped himself on the cheek.

The dwarf continued. "However, as I was saying earlier, I know where you can get your hands on a real rune-sword. . . ."